D1431837

Rescue Press, Iowa City

Copyright © 2013 Jonathan Blum

All rights reserved

Printed in the United States of America

Design by Sevy Perez

First Edition

ISBN: 978-0-9885873-3-5

Text set in Tisa OT

**RESCUE
+PRESS**

rescue-press.org

ACKNOWLEDGMENTS

Thanks, above all, to my family for their love.

I also can't thank the following people enough: Zoe Kashner, Joyce Racz, Marilynne Robinson, Andrew Porter, Amber Dermont, Holiday Reinhorn, Greg Downs, Wellington Bowler, Kirsten Johnson, Robert Ready, Peggy Samuels, Matthew Goldstein, Laura Ruberto, Michelle Remy, and Kristy Guevara-Flanagan.

And very special thanks to Caryl Pagel and Daniel Khalastchi, as well as to Sevy Perez.

travel $\longrightarrow$ learn hard
son

JONATHAN BLUM

LASTWORD

IF I LEARNED COMPUTERS, like my wife Andi tells me to, really learned them, I'd have more in common with the boy, I know, and all this might not have happened. But that's just it: I shouldn't have to learn computers to have a relationship with my thirteen-year-old son. On the contrary, I am now going to have to keep the boy away from the computer. I am proud of his intelligence, of course, and of how he has apparently mastered certain techniques which, I am told, if applied legitimately, might one day lead to a high-paying and respected job. But there's a lot computers can't teach you—about discipline and decency and how to relate normally to other people. That's why Andi and I have always offered Eric and his half-sisters, in addition to a Jewish education, a choice of healthy, positive activities. Swimming, I've often said, would be a good activity for Eric. I like swimming. You can do it competitively, which builds character, and yet it's not an activity that involves rough physical contact with others, which I know Eric dislikes. You can swim your whole life. Swimming would also help trim some of the fat rolls off Eric's middle, which—if he didn't spend so much time at the computer—he could also accomplish by jogging or exercise at a gym. Eric's half-sisters Renata and Mina swim *and* have plenty of time to mess around on the computer. They do well in school. Neither girl is overweight.

That said, now that Eric has been expelled from Traubman V. Goldfarb K-8 Day School Academy, and now that he's been placed on the "100 Online Haters Beware List" by the Southeast Regional office of the nation's second-leading anti-intolerance watchdog group, and seeing as the Shoshanah Kalstein/Ken Mosher civil liability situation appears only to be getting worse, I have had to do a little soul searching. What do these computer stunts of Eric's mean? Has he been trying to attract my attention in a *negative attention* kind of way? Is this what he thinks it takes to be "cool" within his peer group? Is he simply copycatting what boys with computers all over the country do nowadays starting right after their Bar Mitzvahs? No matter the ifs, ands, or buts, it's not going to be "funny ha-ha look-what-I-can-get-away-with, you people" when Eric winds up in prison next time, like the computer madmen whose mug shots you see on CNN. Some of the blame—personal not legal—I must accept. Parents err: We misjudge risk, underexercise our influence. We don't always know how to get through to our children. Yet even factoring in my shortcomings, things do not add up. Why choose the path where no good can come of taking it? Why push mischief to the extreme? This is not something Eric learned from Andi, and it is not something he learned from me. Sadly, I have begun to fear that Eric's behavior in the past few months may in fact be a destructive trait in his mother (alive in South Florida) now pronouncing itself in him, and I would like to do something while it's still early, maybe send him to an adolescent psych specialist or sit him down with a values clarification coach—but Eric, I think, would resist those suggestions, and Andi says I shouldn't speak negatively of Eric's mother, and so I keep these sorts of thoughts to myself.

The problems, I guess you'd have to call them, began last fall. Till then, Andi and I had never received any *bad* reports on Eric. In the six years we'd had him in Traubman V. Goldfarb, his teachers' main negative comments were that his handwriting and spelling were atrocious and that when asked to speak in class, he would either mumble a response or make incomprehensible puffing noises from the side of his mouth (if you'd call that a negative comment). In class, one of his two close friends, Dickie Schmertz or Little Lowell Simkins, would usually step forward to speak/translate for Eric. In the lunchroom, his half-sister Renata would do the same. During these years—the years after I finally got custody of Eric—Andi and I did all we could to keep him on level with his classmates and to protect him from being teased. We were aware, naturally, that Eric didn't enunciate well in public. I was a stutterer until the fourth grade. The point is, you can *get over things*. We invested in a private speech therapist for Eric and by sixth grade got him caught up. We were aware also of Eric's writing inadequacies and Andi worked long hours with him on his English and Hebrew. By the end of seventh grade we had gotten his grades up to one C and the rest B's and A's. Things looked potentially good for college.

Eric's Bar Mitzvah fell in late September, when many of the other kids in his class had already had theirs. Eric, I know, did not look forward to the Bar Mitzvah. He would say it was only going to be a letdown for everyone. Eric is a little shy, and like me, I suppose, prefers to avoid large gatherings. Then there was the whole public speaking aspect of the Bar Mitzvah that he wanted no part of. Still, some things you have to do, a Bar Mitzvah is one of them, and Eric understood that. His attitude, I would say, was overall very positive.

We fitted Eric for a suit. I shopped with him for a tallis. Andi practiced the box-step with him in the family room, in case he might want to ask a girl to slow dance at his dinner party. Now Eric, it should be said here, is what you might call a physically mature but not-quite-caught-up-with-his-age-group-in-certain-other-ways sort of boy. He reached puberty on time. There's nothing wrong with him developmentally. He's of average to above-average height. He has a nice broad chest, though it slopes inward slightly and the pink breasts sag. He has my father's solid shoulders (minus the years of heavy lifting and carrying, which gave Dad's shoulders their great masculinity). He has hair coming along in all the right places. All told, he's not the worst looking kid in the world. Still, he's awkward, a little clumsy physically. And, as has been mentioned, he is chubby. By the standards of the American Medical Association, obese. Not grotesquely obese. But he could do something about his weight. He ought to do something. People judge each other based, in part, on looks. That's not my opinion, it's the way of the world. Your appearance affects what kind of friends you're likely to attract. Not many girls came to Eric's Bar Mitzvah.

Three girls, in fact, stiffed Eric—and our family. These were Shira Lichler, Alison Abramson, and Devi Kreuzer, girls who had been in class with Eric since we started him at Traubman V. Goldfarb, each a little more advanced than Eric socially, a little more precocious, yet girls he'd led "Ein Kelohainu" with on Shabbos mornings, taken van rides with to youth conferences and Disney World retreats, girls a little more popular and confident than he, yes, with pleasant singing voices, good-looking parents, etc., but who had RSVP'd that they would come to his dinner party (Shira Lichler and Alison Abramson both selected chicken for their entrée, Devi Kreuzer salmon: Andi still has the dropback cards) and then did not show up. The head friends-table, draped with a blue-glittered ERIC'S SIMCHA CELEBRATION sign, turned out to be almost empty of girls. At one point I had to take my son aside and say, "What did you do, scare all the girls away?"

A couple mornings later, it occurred to me that I should feel humiliated the three girls hadn't shown up, and I told Eric to get an explanation from them this week, or I would get one from their parents. That night in the family room, Renata turned up with the explanation, delivering it to Andi and me with her usual seriousness—the seriousness that sometimes makes me call her Scout. Her younger sister Mina, the more physically attractive, you'd have to say, of our two daughters, was standing back at the Israeli-tiled wall mirror, carefully barretting her light, thin hair. As per usual, Eric was shut in his room.

First thing that morning, Renata told us, when Eric walked into class, Shira Lichler, Alison Abramson, and Devi Kreuzer, the ones who'd skipped his party, flipped down the mail-order catalogs they'd been looking in and spun halfway round in their seats, putting on sad faces and singing out across the room, "Sorry, Eric! Sorry," that they had all gotten sick during services Saturday morning and had had to run over to Devi Kreuzer's after *oneg* and throw up. For three hours. Which was why they couldn't come Saturday night. "We're sorry we were so sick," they sang. "It wasn't our fault. We almost needed antibiotics. Please forgive us? Please? We still got you presents."

Andi tipped her head back to a spot on the wall just below where she hangs the straw peasant hat I picked up for her for peanuts two summers ago, at a mandibular reconstruction conference in Hong Kong.

"How did Eric respond?" she asked.

Renata's ankles locked. "Probably he just sat with Dickie and Lowell. He wouldn't say anything back, I don't think."

"That's the right thing," Andi said. "Let the others be the small ones."

"That's right," Mina echoed, in what I thought meant agreement. But then she exploded into laughter and began clapping her knees as if her mother's comment were the most preposterous thing she'd ever heard. "Let the others be the small ones," she cackled, and, finishing up the laughter, skipped out of the room, rebarretting her hair.

I had been ready to put the whole dinner party incident behind me and move on with eighth grade, but now I saw I had no choice but to phone up Bernard Lichler, Shira Lichler's father, who is cantor at our synagogue. Shira, according to Renata, was ringleader of the girls. I called from my office the next day. When Cantor Lichler picked up the line, politely I asked was he aware that Saturday night his daughter and two of her friends stiffed my son at his Bar Mitzvah party, then followed up that performance with an insincere and degrading apology? He said he wasn't sure, he hadn't heard, he'd look into what had happened. I said, "I'll tell you exactly what happened," and proceeded to do just that. (Personable though he may be—with his red sideburns, his handembroidered Bukharan kippot, his highly melismatic interpretations of nusach, and a speaking voice my own wife once described as "richer than caramel"—you must spell out word for word anything you want from Bernard Lichler, or you risk getting no results from the man.)

"If my daughter owes your son an apology," he told me, "I will make sure that she gives him one."

"She's *already* given him one, remember?" I said. "*That's* what I'm calling you about."

About three weeks later, Eric's new souped-up computer began arriving in the mail, component by component. I had let him buy a whole new system off the Internet with his Bar Mitzvah money. He had promised it would help him get better grades.

"I still want an hour a day of exercise from you," I said, as we drove one evening to pick up his sisters at the Jewish Community Center pool.

"Does waiting outside class for T.B.S. to show up, then shooting at them with a homemade slingshot count as exercise?" he asked.

"What's T.B.S.?"

"Triple Bitch Supremo. Shira, Alison, Devi."

I cracked a laugh.

"I thought Renata told me last week those girls finally gave you a proper apology, face to face."

"I can still hate their guts."

"Why would you waste your hate on them?"

"Somebody needs to."

"Not you."

"Then who?"

"Forget about them. Just concentrate on you doing well in school. Put them out of the picture."

"Except they always have to be in the picture. They think they *are* the picture."

"So what else do you want from them, Eric? You want Alison Abramson to take you behind the bushes and tongue-kiss you in her tennis skirt and make it all feel better?"

"Idiot," he snarled, and looked out his own dark window.

"T.B.S.," I repeated, liking the ring of it. "I don't think Andi will like that name. Better watch your mouth around her," I said.

Eric got the whole computer set up right before Meet the Parents in the Sukkah Night. I remember because he wanted to stay home and make a list of everything his computer could do that Dickie Schmertz's and Lowell Simkins's couldn't.

"If you've got nothing to do but screw around on the computer," I told him from the office, "you might offer to lift a finger and help your mother with a house-chore."

"She's not my mother," he said.

"Help her anyway."

"Why do we pay a housekeeper twice a week?" he said.

I lowered my voice and said, "If my father, who broke his back so that you and me could have a comfortable life, lived to see me raise a spoiled son, he'd pop me a good one on the lip and then he'd pop you a good one."

Meet the Parents in the Sukkah Night has never been a favorite occasion of mine, and I couldn't really blame Eric for trying to get out of it. Typically you stand around the school sukkah for an hour and a half with three hundred other people, sipping white wine from tiny plastic cups, making polite conversation, avoiding the couples you need to avoid but overhearing them anyhow, bragging about their children's intelligence and test scores. If you already know your children's teachers, which Andi and I generally do, the whole night is a waste of time. You and the teacher exchange words about the coming year's curriculum, she says something nice about your child, you say yes we're very proud of the child, and in a matter of minutes you have wandered off to an out-of-the-way bench, where you can escape the yammer about development community maintenance fees, the rising cost of platinum, and the mess up in Washington, and if you're lucky, catch a look at the Gentile secretary with the knockout hips who works in the office and can usually be seen walking around near the chapel at these kinds of events.

This night was different. Eric's Hebrew/Bible/Siddur/Israel-Interconnectedness teacher Shoshanah Kalstein was new to the school and not everyone had met her—including Andi and me. When we arrived, friends of ours were talking about how warm and energetic she seemed. About how she had just moved home to our city after living in the north of Israel for seven years, and was single and a darned nice catch. One person in the group had heard a rumor that Miss Kalstein had some *issue* that led her to move home. The others didn't want to hear speculation. "*Lashon hara,*" a friend of Andi's from the Jewish Women's Peace Coalition said. "Herb and I already met her. She's gold." Renata pointed her out to me.

You could see right away that the woman had a real personal charm to her. She circled the back of the sukkah in a long dress with a brightly stitched applique frontpiece, greeting parents, smiling generously, pulling back from her ears her black curly hair, then letting the veil of hair fall back open where it had been. Her whole manner of being seemed to make people feel at home. She moved lightly. The movements were unforced. It was as though she had not outgrown a stage of innocence.

When I mentioned to Eric on the lawn that I had just seen Shoshanah Kalstein for the first time, he didn't twitch a muscle.

"She's a jar of honey, wouldn't you say?"

His face did not move.

"Don't tell me you have a crush on her," I purred in his ear.

"Stop," he said, "*now*," and punched me in the arm.

As the evening went on—and the blood rushed to Eric's ears each time I whispered into them his teacher's name—families kept following around Miss Kalstein, who always seemed to be decked by paper chains and lanterns, hanging fruits and vegetables. And as she spoke, I would see her dark-golden fingers squeeze a male student's shoulders from behind, or pull lightly at the father's sleeve. After a while, I began to question this affectionateness. It's one thing to endear yourself, but her displays brought to mind the creeping desperation you'll often see in unmarried, childless Jewish women in their early to mid-thirties. How often they will *touch* and *hug*. *Look receptively* into men's eyes for three to five seconds, then glance away. Paint on red lipstick. What, I found myself asking, is a thirteen-year-old boy supposed to make of having this sort of teacher in the classroom? I am not saying Shoshanah Kalstein crossed a line that evening. Nor am I suggesting that she deserved what was later done to her and Ken Mosher. I am saying she was provocative. She made a provocative impression on me. After we were introduced, the first thing she said was, "I like your shirt, Dr. Langer. It's linen?"

And I said, "Slovakian flax. And please call me Kip. Are those flowering sabras you've got on your dress?"

The rest of fall semester Eric gave only positive reports about school. And maybe it was positive—his grades were on the incline. He didn't seem unhappy. He loved the new computer, that's for sure. Would be on it for hours with Dickie and Lowell, the three of them emerging from Eric's bedroom speaking their own computer language practically, full of acronyms and abbreviations, technical expressions, Eric with a pink glow on his face—dreamy, fatigued, pleased.

Times I managed to catch him alone, I would ask, "How are things coming along in Miss Kalstein's class?" or "You need me to go in there and straighten out Miss Kalstein for you?" and he would say that she was *nice*, or that he *liked her*, or that class *wasn't as bad as it could be*.

"What about T.B.S.?" I'd ask. "They're not giving you any trouble, right?"

"They're stuck-up ho's," he'd say, "but that's normal for them."

Then I'd look over his math and science homework. Or he'd show me the maps he was drawing of Jewish dispersion from Palestine, 597 B.C.E. – 73 C.E. Or he'd talk with Andi about themes from a novel he was reading, and she would test him on vocabulary words and their antonyms. He and Mina rarely hid foreign substances in each other's food or called each other names—*termite, hippo*. Other than the fact that Eric still wasn't exercising enough, he seemed to be doing fine.

Then one schoolnight in early December, toward the time I like to have all lights out, I walked into his room.

"Don't take another step," he said, then tapped some keys on the keyboard and clicked his clicker. He swiveled around, stayed at his computer. "Was that a closed door?" he said.

"Listen, Weisenheimer. It's time to bellyflop yourself into bed.

I know you're not still up doing schoolwork."

"What if I am," he said. "Wouldn't it be tragic if I showed up to school with it not done?"

"You're right," I said. "The tragedy of you getting grounded next semester for dropping your grades."

He made a few more clicks at his computer, removed a disk from the tower.

"What are you still here for?"

The decoration of his room—the potted amaryllis in the corner, the midnight blue sheets, the white quilted comforter, the satin man-in-the-moon that hangs from invisible fish line over the foot of his twin bed—is all Andi's work, and I got lost appreciating how generous with herself my wife has always been to this child of my first marriage.

Since I was already in his room, I reminded Eric that next Saturday night was the Southern States Metro Synagogue Youth 7-9 grade social, and that I didn't think it would kill him to go. I would pay for his ticket. Renata and Mina would be out that night too, painting banners for their monthly *bichur cholim* visit to the skilled nursing facility.

"No thank you very much."

"Hey," I chirped up. "How do you know if you don't try? You might get lucky and find a real girlfriend-in-the-flesh. They're a lot better than the ones on the screen."

That was when he yelped, "Get out of here right now!" and "You don't know anything!" and even, thrusting himself out of the chair, sending it rolling back into the bed, "I hate you, Dad. Seriously. Okay? Hate."

My kid's already four inches taller than me.

"What in hell are you talking about?" I said. "Hate me for what?"

"I don't need a reason," he said, with a crack in his voice. He wiped at an eye with the heel of his hand. His forehead was moist and he was seizing breaths. "You can't make me something I'm not," he squeaked. "All right? I told you. Are you satisfied?"

By then the kid was blubbering a little, choking it back in, and I didn't know what to do.

I stepped closer but not too close. His hands were tensed at his sides like they were cramming something downward.

"Hey, I get you, guy," I said. "You big strong guy. You don't have to dance with anybody you don't want to dance with. Forget the social. All right? Doesn't make a bit of difference to me."

This inflamed the crying and brought more tears.

"Please—" he said, his cheeks now red. "Just go away."

He lumped himself back down in the chair that had rolled away from the computer desk.

"I'm not going to leave things like this," I said. "If I need to understand something, teach me. I'm not too old to learn a new trick."

"It's not you," he then said, frowning. "It's me."

This I didn't get at all.

He stared at the floor, pressing down his light brown hair to one side. The kid was fat. I hated to see it. Fat thighs. Fat ankles. You've got to make the most of what God gives you. The longer he didn't talk to me, the more it got me agitated. I try not to compare the boy to Irene in South Florida, but her spirit was in the room.

"Come on, boy, let's quit talking like this," I said. "Let's go have some ice cream. You want some ice cream? Your mom picked out three new quarts today. You can start your diet tomorrow."

"She's *not my mom*," he cried.

"But she loves you like one," I said, and then I got him to quit crying and go downstairs with me and we sat across the table and had a bowl each together.

January is the month I would take back. If I'd dealt with things better in January, there might not have been a February and there certainly wouldn't have been a March.

The year started normally enough with our annual Killington ski vacation with my in-laws. Eric was mopey—which was to be expected. He doesn't care for downhill skiing, never has. And yet I had the feeling he was mopey this year not because I was pressuring him to ski or use the indoor pool and spa facilities but because he was away from the computer—which personally offended me, and offended me on behalf of my in-laws, who pay for half the trip. Hours each day he read computer magazines. When he wasn't crouched over one of these, he was whispering on his cell phone with Dickie and Lowell, or else lying flat on the carpet, doing nothing. One evening he lay beside the wall like a cadaver, staring upward, while the rest of us ate chips and watched something on cable. I'd had enough. Kneeling beside him and stroking his hair, I pressed a finger into his belly button, saying, "You miss your girlfriend, don't you?" and "You really wish your girlfriend was here, huh, boy." Mina at the end of the couch saw where this was headed. She flapped her arms and crowed off-key, "The computer's Eric's girlfriend! Eric's married to his loving computer!" until Andi stopped her with, "Is that nice? Is that how you would want to be spoken to?" and Renata added, "Just because some people think you're adorable—which you're not—doesn't mean you get to say whatever you want." Eric locked himself in the bedroom. Renata cried "Please, Eric?" but he wouldn't let her in. Andi, taking my elbow, told me to be kinder to my son. I said kindness is one thing, kindness is good. But when you're on a ski vacation with family, you can go a week without your computer. You can play with the team.

We got back on the seventh. A week and a half later, a Thursday, first-semester report cards arrived in the mail. This was the day Rhondalee Abramson, Alison Abramson's mother, called Rita Cohen-Suzuki, principal of Traubman V. Goldfarb, at about one o'clock, saying that she was on her way over to pull her two children out of school—and that Abramson contributions to the Building Fund, the Memorial Fund, and the Youth Opportunity Fund would cease, effective immediately. Twenty minutes later, from what I have heard, Rhondalee Abramson parked in a fire zone near the playground and flicked on her hazards. Then, dressed in a fleece-lined suede coat, wrists clacking with gold hoops, with curled eyelashes and streaked combed-back hair, she burst into Renata's fourth grade classroom, grabbing her son Andy and his correction-fluid-graffittied knapsack, marched down to Eric's class, muttering "L'hitraot, l'hitraot" to no one in particular, and fetched Alison.

She was pulling one child with each hand toward her gold S.U.V., when Rita Cohen-Suzuki, the principal; Vashti Glick, the administrator; and Janet Greenberg, the school psychologist stopped her in front of the chapel. Teachers and students began to catch up, and before long fifty people, including Renata and Eric, were on the scene, surrounding the Abramsons with a sea of inquiring eyes.

Rhondalee Abramson took out a sheet of paper from her gold-clasped purse and unfolded it. It was, as we are all now aware, Alison Abramson's first-semester report card. She held it to Rita Cohen-Suzuki's nose. While Rita Cohen-Suzuki examined the report card through chained Franklin eyeglasses, Rhondalee Abramson growled phrases under her breath like, "Truly incensed" and "Never—*ever.*" A giggle broke from Dickie Simkins. When the principal finished, she gave no indication of what she had read but simply called through cupped hands, "*Talmidim, talmidot.* Time to go back to your classrooms. Everyone. *Maher, maher.* With your teachers. Let's go." Then quietly she asked Shoshanah Kalstein to come to her office after school, and she asked Mrs. Abramson please to attend that meeting.

None of my kids told me that evening what had happened at school. I don't know that I would have listened much anyway, I was so steamed about Eric's grades. They were the worst since I'd gotten custody of him: C in English, C in math (math!), D in Israel-Interconnectedness. No A's. Now he was not even going to get into a state school. To top it all, Shoshanah Kalstein had typed the bizarre remark *You are my favorite soldier I can hardly wait just because you* in the Teacher's Comments column next to the D she'd given him.

I rapped on his door.

"Did you not hand in your final paper on the Partition Plan and the War of Independence? Which I let you research on the Internet instead of making you sit in the library? Open up," I shouted. "D is for Dead Meat."

He cracked the door. He did not look upset or fearful. He plucked the sheet from my fingers.

"I knew she'd do something like this to me," he groaned. "She wants to hurt me."

Over the weekend, I learned that Eric's report card was only one of many that had gone out with strange comments by Miss Kalstein. Next to Dickie Schmertz's Bible grade was the message, *I like you second best try to be harder*. Next to Lowell Simkins' Siddur grade: *He plays the lute and trumpet frequently*. Next to both boys' Israel-Interconnectedness grade: *Arra-ha Arra-ha Boo-boo-bee-doo*. Peculiar comments had gone out on girls' report cards too. By early the next week parents of at least five female students had phoned in to complain about a comment their daughter had received.

That Thursday, late in the afternoon, an emergency faculty/parent Conference of Concern was held to address the report card situation. I had to reschedule two consultations—I've got a successful orthognathic surgery practice—but I made it to the school office fine, five minutes early, in fact. No seats were left in the meeting room, so I went and stood behind my wife Andi—the better, I soon discovered, to keep an eye on Rhondalee Abramson, Uti and Bernard Lichler, Bobbi Kreuzer, and other parents of girls in Eric's class, who were huddled on the opposite side of the table, somehow closing ranks. On our side of the room were parents of eighth grade boys: Andi and me, Faye and Lazaro Schmertz, Bonnie Simkins, and a couple other mothers, one a divorcee from Jacksonville named Fran Westenthal whose son Brent, a national Maccabiah diver, Eric can't stand. The women were convivial, talking about how to organize a schoolwide Get Our Grandmothers Online Day. Even Lazaro Schmertz, the baggy-eyed rug and furniture importer, seemed light-hearted. I was not. The longer I stood, the more tense and suspicious I became. Someone, I could not stop thinking, was about to get sniped here.

The walls of the room were tight and low. Three slim bars of glass gave the only view out. Lining the walls were proverbs, two dozen or so, that the fourth grade class had written out in block lettering on blue-lined paper and framed with construction paper as a gift to Dr. Cohen-Suzuki: "You Can Lead a Horse to Water, But You Can't Make Him Drink," "If You Will It, It is No Dream," "People Who Live in Glass Houses Shouldn't Throw Stones," "A Wise Son is a Joy to His Father." To my left, below "A Stitch in Time Saves Nine" and "Judge Everyone Favorably," Eric's math and sciences teacher Reuvain Pfefferbaum silently marked papers. Ken Mosher, the song-leader, sat beside his guitar case. And Vashti Glick, the administrator, was stuffed into the last chair in the row. Alone at the front of the room was Janet Greenberg, the psychologist.

At last Rita Cohen-Suzuki came in, wearing a brown turtleneck with a jeweled dove-and-olive-branch stickpin at the base of the neck, followed by Shoshanah Kalstein in blue jeans. Miss Kalstein surfed her way behind the girls' parents' chairs to a spot in back of Ken Mosher. She had a ruffled smile. Her dark eyes were solemn. Her backside—which I'd never pictured seeing in jeans—hung unusually low, like a pendant. When she glanced my way, I raised eyebrows and nodded ambiguously, not knowing if she was friend or foe.

"Do we need more chairs in here?" Rita Cohen-Suzuki asked.

"No, no," Miss Kalstein and I replied.

Rhondalee Abramson was, by now, wriggling anxiously in her seat. Cantor Lichler, who had on a studious expression—everything is a performance with him—was waving a little black wand over a hand-held electronic appliance. Andi sent me an affirming grin.

"People," Rita Cohen-Suzuki began, "as you know, we've been finding serious problems with the eighth grade report cards. Wrong grades, teacher comments not made by the teacher. We're very concerned."

On a board, she scribbled the words CONCERN and SOLUTION, then drew a vertical line between them. Rita is a slim little gal in her early 60s from Brooklyn, New York, with pinched features and short salt-and-pepper hair, whose turtlenecks and wool skirts always reek of pipe-tobacco—quite an example, I'd say, to set for children.

"We believe," she continued, "that someone entered the school's computer network without authorization—in other words, broke in—and altered the report cards. We have a technical person looking into exactly what may have happened."

Vashti Glick, the administrator, began to shake her head approvingly.

"Tell when it had to have happened," she said.

"*If* this was a break-in," Rita went on, glancing at her notes, "it would have had to occur sometime after teachers keyed in their final grades and comments and before Vashti printed out report cards last Tuesday the 16th. In other words, over the Martin Luther King holiday weekend."

In every quarter, people began to talk. Shoshanah Kalstein said something imploring in Vashti Glick's ear. The girls' parents made a semicircular jury of themselves. Faye Schmertz asked Andi how well, in general, she *got* computers. Only Reuven Pfefferbaum remained silent, grading papers.

Rita Cohen-Suzuki swung her eyes around the room, one finger pointed at the word SOLUTION.

Lazaro Schmertz's hand shot up. "What do we *know* here, Rita?" he asked. "What is *fact* and what is speculation?"

Rita waited for those whispering to stop.

"We know Shoshanah did not write the comments on these report cards," she began, ticking off a thumb. "And we know grades were changed—not only Shoshanah's but Reuvain's and others'. As to who did this, how it was done, and why? I'm told the person would have had to have a fair amount of computer expertise and a lot of determination. Given the nature of the behavior, we suspect the individual was from within the Traubman V. Goldfarb community—or with a direct tie to our community. Beyond that—"

"So if I hear correctly," Lazaro Schmertz said, "we don't *have* facts. We have suspicions. Is that why we're here? To air our personal suspicions? I took the afternoon away from my business for what purpose?"

Rhondalee Abramson made a stop-the-music motion. She brushed off her slacks and leaned in over the table. Her angora chest faced Andi and me but her eyes peered at Lazaro Schmertz.

"Rita," she said. "I'm sure this busy gentleman will appreciate, and all of us will, if we skip the polite chat and cut to what's real." Her fingernails clattered along the table like advancing hoofbeats. "We know who did this. You told me you agree."

"Who?" snapped Bonnie Simkins.

"In fact, Mrs. Abramson, we don't know," Janet Greenberg the psychologist said, reclining in a green suit. "That's the puzzle we're trying to piece together."

"The girls were who got targeted," Bobbi Kreuzer with braces said.

"The hell they were," Lazaro Schmertz answered. Red had risen to his face. "You want to read my son's?"

He stamped Dickie's report card, like an ante, on the center of the table.

"Mine too," said Fran Westenthal.

Bonnie Simkins threw Lowell's report card on top of the other two.

"Evasions," Rhondalee Abramson muttered.

"What!" I cried. "You think you know who did all this?"

"I'd say your son is one," she said.

"Hold it," said Andi.

"The girls have *all told* me—"

"What girls?"

"My daughter Alison. And her friends. Have all told me. Okay? That since last year. Your son. Has gotten more and more into computer games and computer monsters and outer-space computer-warrior something-or-whatever. Stuff. I don't have to understand it. Okay? Fighting games. He sits right in back of the classroom between subjects and does it. On the school computers. And don't think it's just me who thinks he's a little off. Okay? It's the teachers. It's a lot of people. Am I right, Shoshanah?"

Eyes shot to Miss Kalstein, who held her word. Rita Cohen-Suzuki tried to bring back order, but Andi was hot.

"Ma'am, you'll need to stop speaking this way about our son," she said. "Because my head's starting to boil. Does Eric like computers? Yes, every 13-year-old boy in America likes computers. Most girls, too. But to go from saying a boy likes to play games on the computer to accusing him, for no reason, of hacking? Which basically means breaking the law? I think the one who's a little off here is you."

From a pocket inside her pink angora V-neck, Rhondalee Abramson pulled out Alison's report card. She unfolded it like a pretty girl with pretty fingers in a pretty chair who's been told all her life how pretty she is. "Does this sound familiar?" she said, staring at Andi and me, eyelashes and streaked hair and gold rings and all. "And I quote: 'Israel-Interconnectedness grade: A+++. Comment: *Alison enjoys flagpoles blue and white are her favorites please enjoy them with her. She likes being a S.U.T.B.S.N.1.H and she yum special me slurp.*'"

"Never heard a word of that in my life," I said. "Sounds like every other crackpot comment going around."

"Except no it's not," Rhondalee Abramson said icily. Her fingernails were clattering the tabletop again. "Because my daughter. And other girls. Don't like the way your son looks at them. In class. Okay? Alison has personally told me. More than once. That when the teacher's teaching, your son, on the other side of the room, stares at her, in a half-awake frame of mentality, with his mouth open, drooling. Slurp."

No one on our side of the table knew what to say.

"Cantor Lichler," Rhondalee Abramson said formally, seating herself.

Bernard Lichler stuck away his little wand and gadget, unfolded his daughter Shira's report card, then rose to his full height in the slow, deliberate manner he uses when standing to lead our congregation in prayer. In a rich, stern counter-tenor he recited, *"The cow jumped over the moon yow yow fuzzly ohh all the way home to poppy meow."*

Lazaro Schmertz restrained a chuckle. Cantor Lichler, who is over six feet tall and widely viewed in our community as a handsome and charming man, looked across at me bitterly.

"May I express *my* concern?" I demanded of Principal Cohen-Suzuki, putting a hand on my wife's shoulder and glaring back at the accusing faces on the opposite side of the table. Lichler sat. "Who here can tell me why," I said, "at a Jewish Day School, that teaches Jewish values and history, a history that includes centuries of blame and persecution based on nothing but pure hatred, and costs $18,700 a year per student—why is my son being scapegoated? In this room, at this moment." My fingers were trembling. "Is it that we don't know what really happened and we need to blame someone, so we'll just kick around Eric Langer? The easy target? The not-so-popular boy? I mean, for crying out loud," I said, looking at the parents of Dickie Schmertz and Lowell Simkins, "how many people out there play on computers?"

"There's no question," the psychologist agreed.

"Not to mention that Eric's report card got changed, too," Andi added.

"And if my kid's such a grand wizard on the computer," I exclaimed, "why didn't he change his own grades to something higher than a C in math and a D in Israel-Interconnectedness? He's grounded for those grades."

"I didn't give him a C in math," Reuvain Pfefferbaum said. In the same breath Shoshanah Kalstein said, "I didn't give him a D in Israel-Interconnectedness."

"A *lot* of people out there play with computers," Bonnie Simkins said, tucking her fists under her elbows. "That's all our family has to say."

Shoshanah Kalstein swallowed a deep breath. The tilt of her chin gave a pained expression.

"I need to set this straight," she said, standing against the wall, her right shoulder below "Do Unto Others As You Would Have Them Do Unto You." She was staring at my forehead but did not seem to see anything. "I'm not blaming Eric Langer," she said. Her eyes moved to Rita Cohen-Suzuki. "I'm not blaming anyone. It's just, I want to do a good job at this school. I thought last semester went really well. I like the students here. I like you all. But this situation that's arisen—it's upsetting to me, you know?" Her lips stiffened. "Like being attacked somehow. I have a reputation, a professional reputation. I don't want it to be ruined."

"It's not going to be," Vashti Glick said. Ken Mosher the song-leader added a similar assurance.

The next night I told Eric I wanted to know everything he knew about the changing of the report cards, even if it meant turning in one of his friends. We were out on the short lawn that climbs to the opening of the woods in back of the house. He said he didn't know anything about the report cards. Just that some were pretty funny, his kind of was.

"You didn't do it, in other words?"

His fleshy eyes narrowed.

"Don't lie to me," I said.

He grunted that he was going back inside and took two big steps toward the laundry room door. On the third step, the motion detecting security light caught him in its blaring white gaze.

"Gotcha," I said.

He stood there in the wide-open eye of the light, not moving forward or back, like a person stuttering, or afraid to not talk right.

"Come on, bandit," I laughed. "Stand a few more seconds with your pop. Is it the worst thing?"

He sulked up the lawn.

It was a warm winter evening, and we were turned not quite toward one another.

"I'm not blaming you," I told him, facing the high woods. "I'm asking."

"Asking what?" he said, a slight crack in the voice.

"Because adolescents pull stunts," I said. "I pulled stunts. I screwed up plenty in junior high, you're old enough to know. Mouthing off. Trying to get attention from the pretty girls. But if your friends and you did pull some kind of stunt, I need to know now so we can take appropriate prophylactic measures."

The bare tops of the tulip poplars were daubed with a quiet light.

"I don't know you," he said.

A thrush sang out. Two thrushes. One finished the other's sentence. The one couldn't wait for the other to stop.

"You hear that?" I said. "What do you suppose those two are saying?"

The motion detecting light burned back off. It was next to silence. Just a scrabbling of leaves.

"'How did we get stuck up next to this house?'" he mumbled. "'Where did we take a wrong turn and end up here?'"

After shul the next day I again asked my son: "Tell me what you know. I won't be angry if you played a part. Let's just handle it, you and me, before it goes any further."

The edges of his lips curled down, and after pausing a long while, he said, almost as if I was too clod-headed to be spoken to, "Do you understand that getting into that system would not be hard? Seriously. Do you understand that? A monkey could get in there. Any medium-smart monkey who felt like it would be capable. He'd just have to look around for holes in certain blocks of numbers and then poke his finger through. Monkey-monkey-monkey. But covering your tracks, so nobody would know who'd been in there? *That* would take a smarter monkey."

"So you're saying you didn't do it but a monkey did?"

"I'm saying, Why do I ever talk to you?"

The last day of January, Andi and I received a handwritten report card from Eric's teachers, showing that he had gotten a 3.25 the previous semester, his best marks ever, and not a 2.5, as the false report card had indicated. I leaped with joy. Every wrong decision I had made dating back thirty-five years felt somehow vindicated. Eric might even *choose* his college. I lifted his restrictions and told him that as far as I was concerned, the whole episode with the report cards was water under the bridge.

"Keep doing what you've been doing," I said. "Lock yourself on the Internet. Crowd around the screen with your buddies. Play with that joystick."

My troubles felt diminished by an order of magnitude.

The following afternoon, a fifth-grade boy from a local public school was brought into my office. A classmate had knocked him unconscious the day before during gym class. He'd received three blows, producing two fracture lines on the left side of the jaw, the loss of two lower molars, and serious swelling. He was a small kid with a close-cropped haircut, not from our part of town, and though I see jaw fractures, even multiple jaw fractures, all the time, something about the expression in his eyes—absent, almost as if the eyes had no understanding of what the jaw knew perfectly—shook me up and even sickened me a little. The bullying at public school, I guess it was: things I'd seen and been through, that my father had seen and been through, that I had done everything in my power to protect my own son from. I secured the kid's jaw with titanium screws and plates, told him in six to eight weeks he would be as good as new, and clapped a five-dollar bill in his palm to go take his mom for a milkshake. I drove home counting my kids' blessings.

The next few days, I felt like I was on some kind of win streak—the way I was handling things with my children, my marriage, and my patients. When Mina got nipped on the cheek by a cocker spaniel at a friend's birthday party and broke out screaming at home that she needed plastic surgery or she would never look perfect again, driving Eric to chase her around the kitchen island with a tequila bottle, threatening to *really damage* her face, I clamped his wrists behind his back and said to him, "Do we pay attention when you have moods? Do we let you be unhappy in peace?" afterwards kissing Mina's tiny indentations, telling her that she was far better off than the boy I'd met whose mouth was filled with plates and screws, and promising that in three days max she would look as lovely and photogenic as she always had.

Or at dinner, when Andi announced that Renata did not make a viola chair in the All-Metro Under-12 Youth Orchestra, I cheerfully—and with what I thought was the right note of crestfallenness—

reminded everyone that Renata was only nine and that next year she was a lock for viola. In the bedroom Andi informed me I was not treating Renata's disappointment seriously enough, first saying Eric's aren't the only problems in this house, then letting me know I wasn't paying enough attention to *her* either. So I called a babysitter and took my wife out Saturday night to a fish restaurant. Told her I loved her, twice. Said, Count on a double bouquet of flowers for Valentine's next week and a fifty-dollar bottle of wine. Next day I told each girl she was number one with me.

By Monday morning, I felt like a fixer. A twenty-year-old microgenia patient on whom I'd done a chin advancement came back for a post-op, satisfied, more than satisfied, telling me she was able to look at herself in the mirror like never in her life. Profile and all. Thank you, Doctor, she said.

I phoned Andi at the Metro Jewish Women's Peace Coalition office, exclaiming, "I tell you, An, it never stops feeling good helping make things better for others."

"True," she said. "You just keep *your* head screwed on straight, okay, Doctor?"

I'll never know what really happened in Shoshanah Kalstein's classroom on Monday, February 12. The way Dickie Schmertz and Lowell Simkins have described it—though who can believe those two any more? who can believe anyone at that school?—Alison Abramson and Devi Kreuzer raised their hands in unison during parshah study and accused Eric of staring at them *inappropriately*—of *sexually harassing* them. Another girl, Beth Kleinoff, said Eric was doing the same to her. She had seen his tongue drip. When Shoshanah Kalstein asked Eric if he'd just been looking at any of the girls in a way he knew he wasn't supposed to, he could not squeeze words out.

Miss Kalstein reportedly then said to Eric, with a pained expression, "I am concerned, really concerned, about the behavior in this class"—though maybe, as she has since claimed, she was saying it to other students, to all the students.

Lowell Simkins answered, "Gveret Kalstein, if Eric ever looks at the other side of the room, he's not staring at the feminoids. He's concerned about the dangerous levels of pollution they emit into the atmosphere. Through their orifices. Which affects all of our fertility and ability to breathe."

Brent Westenthal, the sleek Maccabiah diver, and some other boys hissed and said, "Right. Whatever. Freak."

Then Alison Abramson said, "All I know is? My dad Chuck Abramson is a serious lawyer, and if I wanted him to, he could get Eric Langer expelled from this school *tomorrow*."

"My dad *and* my mom are lawyers," Beth Kleinoff added.

"Can we please behave like young men and women?" Shoshanah Kalstein cried out. "Our *tanachs* are open. We're here to learn. I want to get back to Yitro. I want to get back to the third day at Sinai."

"I know where we were, Gveret Kalstein," Lowell Simkins said. "Moses was teaching an important lesson. 'Be ready. Stay pure. *Al tigshu el isha.*'"

Pretty, blond, bobby-pinned Shira Lichler, in a yellow dress and blue tights, sighed loudly.

"Do you have any idea how to not make yourselves look ridiculous in front of us?" she asked. "It's sad. It really is." The class snickered. Eric's cheeks flushed pink. She continued, "You seriously make me think sometimes, if I—"

"—had a gun, I'd use it on myself," Dickie Schmertz said.

"Point it at your skull," Alison Abramson said.

"Death threat," Lowell Simkins said. "I count," he finger-totaled, "eighteen witnesses."

"Young men," Shoshanah Kalstein pleaded, looking at Eric. "Adult members of the Jewish community. Please cooperate. I don't want to send you to the office. You be the leaders. You set the tone."

"*Us* be the leaders?" Dickie Schmertz said.

Miss Kalstein ran a hand through her hair. The back of her neck seized for a couple seconds. Brent Westenthal asked was she all right, could he get her some bottled water or anything. Miss Kalstein said yes, that would be helpful, and carried on with an even more pained expression.

Eric didn't come home from school. Andi tracked him down at Dickie Schmertz's and brought him home for dinner. He hardly moved a facial muscle except to eat.

"Mouth works well enough to chew but not talk?" I said to him. "Story of our food bill."

"He's free not to join the conversation," Andi said to Eric comfortingly.

"Eric, how much do you hate Alison Abramson?" Renata asked. "Or do you hate Shira Lichler worse?"

Eric didn't answer.

"Maybe the Orthodox have it right," Andi mused. "Boys and girls should be educated separately."

"Which girls?" I said to my son.

"T.B.S.," said Renata.

"Whah?" Andi said.

"Yeah, whah?" Mina said, sticking out her tongue at Eric.

Eric cracked his knuckles.

"T.B.S. are T.F.B.," he said, or rather puffed from the side of his mouth, almost incomprehensibly, in a way I hadn't heard him speak since we finished with the speech therapist. "Basically, T.V.G. is a T.B. factory. Now B.K. licks their C.T.'s for them." He almost sounded drunk or crazy. "I'd seriously have N.P. S.'ing their T's open if there was N.S.T. as J."

"Since when do you speak in code?" Andi asked. "And from the side of your mouth?"

"I understood," Renata said.

"Care to share?" I asked.

Eric half-committingly nodded permission to Renata.

When Renata translated the sentences, Andi looked aghast. Her eyes tried to place where she'd heard this kind of abbreviating before. She stared at me, then realized it was Eric she was talking to.

"I don't want to hear that B word in this house," she said.

"That's what they are to him, Mom," Renata said. "He sees a flat thing with food on it, he calls it a plate. He sees a girl that acts like a B he calls her a B."

"Not in my home," Andi said. "We don't speak about women or girls that way, even in anger. Just like we don't speak derogatorily about African-American people or gay people or any other historically oppressed group. We try to understand and reach out. Not attack."

Eric whispered in Renata's ear.

"'Are spoiled, conceited, nutcrusher Jewish females who get worshipped every day an oppressed group?'" Renata translated. She added, "He's just being honest, Mom. You tell us to be honest."

Andi stood.

"What I'm hearing from you, Eric, disturbs me," she said, looking at me.

Eric's nostrils were twitching, and he appeared pleased to have reached this response. He shoveled another plate of food down, left his dishes in the sink, and went up to his room. I scarcely saw his face for the next two days.

The call from school came in the middle of the afternoon on Wednesday.

"It's time," said Vashti Glick the oversized administrator, provocatively. "We need you to come meet with Rita right now."

She was heaving, almost snorting breaths into the phone. It sounded as if she had been stomping around her desk for ten minutes, practicing an aggressive folk dance.

"We're not all in the eighth grade," I reminded her, "who can just be called into the principal's on a moment's notice."

I backed into the records room of my office, behind the receptionist's wall, away from everyone.

Clenching a fist, I said, "Because Eric?"

Vashti Glick went on heaving breaths into my ear.

"We don't know yet, Doctor," she said. "But somebody has caused two people at this school a lot of grief. A lot of grief and anguish, Doctor."

"What don't you know yet?"

"We don't have proof positive, so I wouldn't say yet into the—"

"*Yet*?" I shouted, and in my swelling indignation I fell back against a file cabinet and had to stop myself from sliding down it.

"Dr. Langer?" she said.

Weak-kneed, almost pedaling for balance, I grabbed a cabinet handle, somewhat dizzily at first, then found myself gazing up along a shelf at the gallery of old before-and-after photos I keep from different jaw repositioning surgeries I've performed through the years. On one mandibular set-back I did as a resident in Tampa almost twenty years ago—a generation!—the patient had signed the after photo, "You're #1, Doc. Don't ever forget." Where had I gone wrong with my son? Having discipline problems at school wasn't the worst thing that could happen to a kid. In college I missed half a term and was nearly kicked out for taking a minor part in a pre-med test cheating ring. It's where you end up, my father always said, that counts. But where was Eric headed? He had no clear direction or ambition to succeed.

The sky through the tall circular skylight looked like a pale, shallow, overturned bowl.

"When are you going to be here?" Vashti Glick demanded.

"I have appointments till 6:30," I told her. "And it's Valentine's Day. I take my wife out for a nice meal."

"Are you aware, Dr. Langer," Vashti Glick grunted, "that Valentine's Day is a holiday of Christian/pagan ancestry? And what if your son hurt real people today on the computer? What would your response be to that? To go out for a romantic meal on a Christian/pagan holiday?"

"You know, you people are crazy," I snapped. "Here you go convicting my son again of accusations with no evidence. You're worse than the *goyim*, you know that?"

"I want to tell *you* something, Dr. Langer. I got an e-mail this morning and so did everyone else at Traubman V. Goldfarb. Including all children old enough to read and operate a computer. I'm not sure yet what's real or what's made up," she said, "but I have a feeling. And when we find out for sure—" Her breath sank. She wasn't heaving breaths any longer. "I just wanted you to know."

"I'll have my wife come in immediately," I said.

At quarter past eight I walked into my home with an armful of roses for Andi and a box of chocolates for each of my daughters. In the dining room I leaned the chocolates against the vase of roses. Then I rearranged the chocolates to lay flat in front of the roses. Leaning the chocolates against the vase seemed best, so I put them back that way. The house felt empty, so I changed and stood up by the woods, but I didn't feel welcome there either. I kept hearing my pulse behind my ear. I pointed a finger toward the motion detecting light over the laundry room door and pow, it went off. A cold wind kicked up. I went back inside and checked for phone messages. Still nothing from my family.

About ten minutes later, Mina scratched at the door, then burst inside, throwing down her bookbag.

"Eric i-his buh-sted," she sang, while she twirled herself through three different rooms. She was wearing a red sweater and red Valentine's Day ribbons, which flapped in her light, thin hair where the barrettes usually hung. "Eric's gonna nee-heed a new-hew ad-dre-hess," she sang to the ceiling, and clapped and stamped her feet rhythmically, like a cheerleader.

"Mina Langer is a liar," Renata called to the same spot on the ceiling. She and Andi had gotten identical haircuts yesterday—the dark brown hair shaped neatly, cut two inches above the shoulder.

Eric lumbered in. Dark blue pants, collared shirt, plaid-lined jacket, he looked like the house scarecrow, knock-kneed, bulbous around the center, head listless and stuffed with foreign material. His hair looked as if it had been rolled out of his scalp and patted down to the side of his *kippah* with displeasure.

Andi followed him in with a scowl I had never seen on her. She threw off her jacket.

"Is it still cold outside?" I asked.

Eric went onto his cell phone and disappeared.

"I want some order in this house," she said.

"Order you shall have," I said.

Mina had disappeared too, leaving Renata, who was sniffing the roses with the responsible expressions of a grown woman.

"You know who one of those chocolates is for," I told her. "Best kind there is."

Andi looked through the mail at the kitchen counter. She did not acknowledge the roses, although their scent was tremendous.

After a few moments, she said, without looking up, "Their only questions are what roles each boy had. Apparently, it was all done right here on Eric's computer last night."

I picked up a long red rose stem below the petals, tested the sharpness of one curving thorn, then made a space behind my canines for the stem. I balanced the rose, grinning.

"Dad," said Renata.

I spat the stem back into my fingers, cutting the inside of my lower lip.

"Would you like to know what's happening?" Andi asked, not having seen my rose balancing act. "Or would you like to pretend it's just going to go away."

"He's my son," I said. "I know what's not going to go away."

The scowl returned. I leaned my left hand next to the vase, and quietly began humming, "Raindrops on roses and whiskers on kittens."

"How about some juice, honey," Andi asked Renata, and poured them each glasses.

"Okay," I said. "Spill it. Just spill it."

I was licking blood and vase-water at the bottom of my mouth.

"Somebody," Andi said, lips tightening. "Or all three of those boys—I can't imagine it wasn't all three—" Her chest and shoulders jerked slightly against the timing of her breaths. "Found their way into Shoshanah Kalstein's e-mail account last night and forwarded all the e-mails between her and Ken Mosher, the song-leader, to every student and faculty member at the school."

"So?"

"So?" she mimicked. "Somebody *broke* into the school's e-mail system. *Invaded* a teacher's personal files. *Went and read* through all her mail. Then *spread* private letters of hers anywhere they pleased."

"You don't know how Miss Kalstein and Mr. Mosher write each other," Renata added.

She turned her face from side to side, making a pair of male and female grownup voices:

me n u 2morow nite shoshi rite?

Chavivi, I'm going to give you a Valentine's Day gift at my place that will make sure you never forget me.

well do it were gonna do it well definately do it ill give u somethin what time u out?

Probably 5.

were still going to solomons folk music club first rite?

YES! We HAVE to. You have to play. You told me you would. You know I love your lips around a harmonica.

rather have them on ur lips.

Happy V-Day, motek.

happy now. happier later.

A laugh broke from my stomach.

"You think this is funny, Kip?"

"Eric's teacher is doing it with Ken Mosher? The pretty boy who wears a bandanna around his leg? She must outweigh that guy by twenty-five pounds," I said.

"What are you saying? In front of our nine-year-old daughter."

"That's not even it, Dad. There's way more."

"It's it for now," Andi said sharply. She stacked the mail. Then, "*You're* what encourages him," she said to me. "You say you disapprove, but you approve. And what about that poor embarrassed woman? How is she going to be able to show her face in school?"

Andi cleared the counter of mail, except for one envelope. I joined her next to the stove. I squeezed both my hands into a thickly padded silver oven mitt, raised the mitt over my head with the thumb high like a big misshapen shark's fin, and began to circle her belt in a romantic way, sniffing at the rose scent from the dining room and making affectionate "Jaws" sounds. The envelope was from Federation.

"Vee must owe them a check by now, don't vee?" I said, in a grinning, night's-not-over, devoted-shark's voice.

"Put that potholder down!" she shrieked.

Renata ran up and held me around the waist.

"I just don't want us to be late with our commitments," I cried, and went and got the wine opener from its spot on the island, thanked Scout for her fine work, and sent her off to her room.

Shoshanah Kalstein did not come to school the next day. Or the next. A substitute was brought in to teach Hebrew/Bible/Siddur/Israel-Interconnectedness but he quit at the end of the week, saying the students did not exhibit basic respect for G-d, each other, or the study of Torah. The following week, Miss Kalstein still was out sick and a fuss began to go up about it. The eighth grade sent a small citrus basket and an oversized we-miss-you card to her. Principal Cohen-Suzuki and Vashti Glick paid visits. Andi worried about Miss Kalstein, said one evening that *we* should send a card, and include little messages of our own. But what if Shoshi had just overdone it on Valentine's Day, I said, burning the midnight oil with Ken Mosher. Folk music club. Candlelight. Touch my feathery hair. Let's go back to your place. Then came down with a bad case of sangria poisoning. Andi was not amused.

"A woman that caring, that open, that loving of children, does not just *bounce back* from being publicly humiliated at her own school."

Andi made sure to say things like that in front of Eric, whose state of mind none of us—not even Renata, I think—really understood. His face was nearly always chubby and inexpressive, unsmiling, willfully silent. I'd say he put on seven pounds the second half of that month, the creased segments of his neck plumping and thickening. When he did speak, it was usually to utter a brief, grudging reply or else string together a few breathy, half-comprehensible sentences, riddled with abbreviations and computer terminology. Either way, the goal was to conceal. When I said so to him, he found my frustration amusing.

"The attacker loves to be the attacked," was one of his favorite expressions. "Pity the less fortunate," was another. And, "Why does the truth bother people so much? It's just the truth."

An admission of responsibility, a square dialogue, an answer to a simple question such as "How much of this was you, how much was the other two?" were not to be had.

Dickie Schmertz and Lowell Simkins didn't come over in the evenings, and I didn't hear Eric talk to them much on the phone. He spent most of his time perfecting his solitude—that is, when I wasn't having him wash the cars or carry the garbage cans to the curb or do sit-ups or perform any number of other routine physical activities that might once and for all set him on the path to self-discipline and good sense. At school, Renata told me, he and Dickie and Lowell were being interviewed one at a time by Principal Cohen-Suzuki. Classmates were being asked what they thought might have motivated these three to "go after Shoshanah Kalstein" (Vashti Glick's expression) this way. The regional chief of computer security at the Anti-Intolerance Alliance was brought in to question the boys about their computer activities and maybe scare some wisdom into them. By February's end, the result was that Eric had enemies—more than we knew. Half the places Andi and I went, we caught a squinting-eye look of some kind: at shul, the JCC, the school parking lot, the mall, Mina's dance and acting lessons, even at a Metro Jewish Women's Peace Coalition fundraising event, where Andi was chair. People—and not just the usual rotten apples of Traubman V. Goldfarb—seemed to hate us. Andi couldn't stand it. Within days she had taken on a way of straightening her shoulders and fixing her gaze when entering a room that told anyone who planned to judge her to back off. Myself, I awaited the nasty glances, and met each with a double and a promise that the accuser would not get the last word. Eric walked with his T-shirt like a target.

I finally agreed to meet with Rita Cohen-Suzuki on Friday, March 2, at 3 p.m., for a Conference of Remedial Alternatives. The school, she guaranteed, had its facts straight, and yes, there was a directly traceable problem involving the use of Eric's home computer on the night of February 13.

"I'll be there," I said, "but God help you all if you are orchestrating another round of public hate-slinging toward my son. He'll take what's coming to him but not an ounce more."

"No one hates here, Kip," she answered, "so please don't say otherwise. We love Eric, and have valued his unique gifts since you first brought him to us. A misdeed has been committed. That's what we need to deal with."

"Just say you taught him," I told her. "Don't tell me you've loved him."

Andi and I met at the top of the office walkway at the zither-shaped concrete bench whose seat spells *Shalom Yeladim* in a mosaic of brilliant-colored stone flecks. Thick clouds hovered low, and the glass entrance to the office, which rises from the pavement like the hull of a green ark, reflected their gloomy shades in hundreds of identically tinted squares. The young neatly planted trees and grilles of cars surrounded us like an angry audience. Inside the office, the mood brightened some. The walls were taped with signs and announcements that shone with the optimism the school is supposed to encourage in the students: bright necklaces of paper hung at a child's eye-level saying, "You Are Special To Us" and *"B'tzalmenu, kidmutenu"*; there were happy reminders of an upcoming afternoon of Sephardic dance, a field trip to a river. How many times had I entered this modern office—that I helped the school build—proud of my wife, my family, my people!

I followed Andi into the conference room, expecting, I don't know why, to see only Rita and Eric. Instead, the Schmertzes—Faye, Dickie, and Lazaro—were spread out where the staff had sat at the January meeting, and the Simkinses—Bonnie, Lowell, and this time Lowell's father Lawrence—were where the parents of the stuck-up girls had sat. Eric sat alone, on our side of the table, half-eyeing the bars of windows.

"Simkins!" I cried, and by the elbows I pulled to his feet my now-ex-investment portfolio manager, Lawrence Simkins. "Taking a break from making us all some money?"

"Education first, Doctor."

"Isn't that the truth," I said. Simkins clapped his littler hand on mine. The man works tremendous hours—including Shabbats, not that that's any of my business—so it was an extra surprise to see him. "You look good for a Republican."

"And you for an overpaid physician."

"Right you are," I laughed. "All the good cost containing your buddies in the HMOs do, keeping the system running smooth and fair, they're the ones who ought to be compensated better."

Simkins gave my left cheek a little rub and Andi's a kiss. He has a thick head of black hair, which he combs straight back. He went to Harvard, an extremely successful person, about four inches shorter than I am. Lowell has his same high forehead.

"Keeping a close eye on your boys?" I asked him and Lazaro Schmertz, who looked like a big butcher of a man today, about to burst the shoulders of his corduroy blazer. "I don't let mine out of my sight any more. I had no idea the troubles I needed to keep my eye out for. I mean, when I was in junior high school, if I told my father I was shut in my room writing a paper on Three Distinguished Jewish Figures in the Sciences, you can bet I was..."

"You're nervous," Andi whispered to me. "Just keep calm."

She led me to our side and seated me next to my son like I was an old blind man. I kissed the side of his head. He smelled like a slightly fragrant oil that no one had detected before. The women talked. I put my palm over my boy's *kippah* and felt the God-given life force I'd felt in him the day he was born. Outside, the passing faces in the office glanced at us like we were animals in a cage.

"Tuck in your oxford," I whispered to Eric.

Rita Cohen-Suzuki marched in with a dark portfolio case, followed by Vashti Glick the administrator, Ken Mosher the songleader, Janet Greenberg the psychologist, and a woman in her mid-twenties with shoulder-length hair who wore an army coat over a black T-shirt that had a large Star of David and the words "Hate Stops with Me" printed over a red octagon. They sat near the board like officials.

As Rita went to close the door, a dutiful-looking child with a funny grin wandered in, pointed up at the proverbs along the wall, and said to Rita, "We made those for you."

"You did, Leah Rafa," said Rita. "And I like them so much, I hung them for everyone to see."

"That was good," said the girl, and left.

Vashti Glick watched this exchange with great satisfaction. The girl's hair had been braided perfectly, like two challahs.

"Justice, justice," I banged the table. "Let's pursue it."

Rita took three files from her dark portfolio.

"Candlelighting," Vashti Glick interrupted, "is at 6:07 tonight, and everyone will be home for it. Let this not be a concern."

Rita invited Lawrence Simkins to be seated. When he said he preferred to stand, Rita, whose slender figure arches forward when standing before a group, then lolls like a much younger woman's, insisted there was no need to stand, and yet Lawrence Simkins stayed standing, a hand resting at the base of his son's neck.

The principal explained that our purpose here was to establish what took place the night of February 13th at Eric Langer's home computer—and who took part. Once we knew that, the proper remedial response could be discussed.

"Where is Shoshanah Kalstein?" I asked.

"Shoshanah might not return to Traubman V. Goldfarb," Rita Cohen-Suzuki said.

Andi shuddered. Ken Mosher regarded Eric and me in what I can only describe as a malevolent fashion.

The gal with the "Hate Stops with Me" T-shirt launched into what she called *the facts of the case.* From her manner, you would have thought she had never come across acts more indecent than the ones she said took place in my home the night of February 13th. Scribbling abbreviations and geometric shapes on the board, she described how an "attacker" (she used this word numerous times, always in the singular) had "compromised" the Traubman V. Goldfarb e-mail server (she seemed to want to cast the computer as a kind of sexual victim) at 10:03 p.m. As she went into detail, mild smiles flitted across the lowered faces of Dickie Schmertz and Lowell Simkins. The gal spoke of a "security hole" in the school's "web server software" that the "attacker" had "exploited," and of the "absence of a firewall," which had made it easier for the "attacker" to "enter remotely" and "execute" "commands."

I listened and listened and didn't want to ask a stupid question, but I didn't want my son getting blamed for acts he did not commit, or did not commit alone, so I asked, "Not that I question your expertise, miss, but how do you know all this went on at *Eric's* computer?"

"You mean, how technically?"

I didn't know what I meant.

"Has he admitted this to you?" I asked. "He hasn't admitted it to me, and he wasn't the only one there that night. My son is not an 'attacker.'"

Lawrence Simkins, standing, evaluated me.

"We know from the IP address," she said, and scribbled some more shapes on the board. "Your computer's IP address IDs where you travel on the Internet. These boys all know this. Say you visit a Web address. Or better, you log in remotely to another computer—for instance, a computer you don't have permission to visit, like the Traubman V. Goldfarb server. Your IP address identifies you. The Traubman V. Goldfarb server will timestamp your login. The attacker may have thought his computer's IP address had successfully been faked—'spoofed,' we call it. It wasn't."

The room took a breath.

"How smart would you have to be to do all of what you're saying was done that night?" I asked. "Getting in and sending the e-mails around and everything. Because my son has never been the best of students. He has not exactly ever shown himself to be an academic genius."

The woman gave no answer.

When I glanced at Eric, he looked remote—and old, older than I. I couldn't tell if he was passing messages through coded facial signals with the two other boys or if they were passing signals without him. Really, I had no idea what was going on between these three boys or how smart any of them were or weren't or what this young computer gal was really saying.

"*Bachurim*," Rita Cohen-Suzuki said, "who is going to tell the true story of what happened that night around the computer?"

"No one," Dickie Schmertz blurted, sadly, and the speaking fell to him.

Dickie has high curly hair, and eyes set apart in a manner that many people would call ugly, and if not ugly, strange. He doesn't really look at you. His parents can't have been pleased. His dress habits and grooming do little to convey that he makes the most of what he has. But as he had always been a loyal friend to my son, with few fights and only brief differences in their six-plus years at Traubman V. Goldfarb, I looked at Dickie the way you look at those who, because they do something good for someone you love, you see differently than you otherwise might, until that choice to see becomes your natural way.

"Tell what happened," Rita Cohen-Suzuki said, bobbing on her back foot.

"You already know," Dickie said. "We were researching our Three Distinguished Jewish Figures in the Sciences. We were learning about our heritage."

"He told you," Lazaro Schmertz said, a vein flaring at his temple. "He wasn't the one."

"What were you doing using remote access software to log in to the school server?" said the Hate Stops with Me gal.

"What was *I* doing?" said Dickie, again sadly—more sadly.

"Who installed that software in Eric's PC?" she continued.

"You'd have to ask Eric," Lowell Simkins replied. "It's his computer."

Lawrence Simkins clapped the back of his son's neck like a victory cheer, then shook out his own shoulders like a fight producer before the next round.

"Did you install it?" the computer gal asked Eric.

He shook his head up and down.

"Alone?"

He continued making his mechanical yes. It went on for a short while.

"Why?" the computer gal asked.

He looked at his fingers.

"It's legal," he said.

"She didn't ask is it legal!" Vashti Glick shouted, springing forward in her layered celestial-colored gown of mall batik. "Is it *right*! We don't do things because they're *legal*! And what you and the others here did, I have news for you, was *not legal*."

"Ma'am, you're out of line," Lawrence Simkins said. "Let these young people tell the story."

I was suddenly so parched I wanted to take a drink of my wife's skin. As sure as a lanky moyel named Rabinovich had pulled up to my house in Tampa thirteen and a half years ago in Ray-Ban sunglasses and a '64 Barracuda and circumcised my boy on a tasseled pillow, this boy of mine was lying. About something. I put my mouth around the soft part of Andi's wrist. She shook it away.

After a few minutes, Dickie and Lowell admitted, when prompted by Lawrence Simkins, that they had helped Eric install the remote access software on Eric's computer. They had taken "some rides around the block" together, visited different "sites of interest."

"Now you're talking," I said to the two boys, and elbowed Eric in a tallowy spot around the ribs. Andi pinched my leg until I quieted.

But both Dickie and Lowell denied adamantly that they had helped Eric break into the school server the night of the 13th or forward any of Miss Kalstein's or Mr. Mosher's e-mails.

"Langer drove," Lowell Simkins said, clasping hands in front of him. "He knows it's true."

"We're not saying we weren't there," Dickie said, congruously, his eyebrows breaking up with moroseness like he had Marfan syndrome. "But we didn't *do* anything."

"We were just on the bed," Lowell said. "Eric knows that's true."

"But neither of you boys," Andi said, peaceably, "who are his best friends, put your foot on the brakes? All three of you knew very well what was going on. You knew you could hurt somebody. You knew what you were doing was wrong and against the rules. Why didn't anyone come forward and be reasonable and stop it?"

"That's what I'd like to know," Faye Schmertz agreed.

As Lazaro Schmertz's face grew bloody with consternation, I couldn't help but notice that Eric was getting some pleasure from these proceedings, watching the ring of spears tighten around him, take aim, and him fleshy at the center.

"Eric," Rita Cohen-Suzuki said, and a hush fell over the room. "Did you commit these acts alone or did the other two boys participate with you? Be specific."

"I didn't need them," he said. He glanced up at his old friends and mumbled something no one understood.

"Say again?" the principal asked.

He didn't repeat himself.

"Say it, boy. Say your peace," I said. "You've got the floor."

The longer he didn't speak, the more contempt I felt he was showing not only for the school—which on some level I could understand, given his not-always-positive experiences there through the years, and this year in particular—but for Andi and me. Handling him by the hair, I pointed his eyes in the direction of the three-part blue-framed proverb over Rita Cohen-Suzuki's shoulder: "If I Am Not For Myself, Who Am I For? If I Am Only For Myself, Who Will Be For Me? If Not Now, When?" Bridling, he shook off my hands.

"Where are we going with this, Rita?" Lazaro Schmertz barked. "My son is a top student. He told you what he did and didn't do. Why am I listening to more of this? Why am I still here?"

Lawrence Simkins, little hips swiveling in his pinstriped suit, indicated that he felt similarly.

By the door I saw Renata and Mina peeking in. I raised a finger not to enter.

Vashti Glick asked who changed the report cards.

Dickie blurted, "Eric?" and began to cry. Eric shrugged. I shouted that if my son did *that* alone, then God still works miracles since there is no way Eric could have spelled half those words correctly.

"Spell check," said Lowell Simkins.

With his neatly combed-back hair and impeccably tailored stare, Lawrence Simkins stood like a bright falcon, untouchable, behind his son.

Vashti Glick was the first to suggest separate punishments for Eric and the other boys—a two-week suspension with no participation in the Purim carnival for Eric, probation and a 500-word essay on not standing by idly while wrong is being done for Dickie and Lowell. The psychologist said she preferred rehabilitation to punishment. The Hate Stops with Me gal wanted punishment. "They knew what they were doing," she said. "They built a pit, and then they fell in it." Ken Mosher sat and seethed, stoking what he no doubt wanted us to see was the ever-burning fire of his devotion to Shoshanah Kalstein.

"My son," Lawrence Simkins said flatly, "is not going to have anything put on his permanent record that could adversely impact his future in any way."

Simkins spoke with an utter lack of insecurity in his voice. The amount he contributes to the school is probably shocking.

Rita Cohen-Suzuki, hands behind her back, raised her eyes over everyone's heads and above the proverbs. She appeared lost in an idea that stretched darkly beyond all of us. She said, "I think everyone in the room needs to be made aware of one other issue that has not yet been mentioned. The school has spoken with a lawyer, who said that *the hacker* may be personally liable for any injuries caused by his actions at the computer against Shoshanah Kalstein and Ken Mosher."

"Who's injured?" Faye Schmertz said.

Lazaro hushed her.

Rita described the variety of intentional torts that this lawyer, a member of our community, said could be brought against the hacker—even if the hacker was in the eighth grade—including those for "Public Disclosure of Private Facts," "Invasion Upon Seclusion," and "Intentional Infliction of Emotional Distress." The hacker, said the lawyer, had engaged in adult conduct and could be held to an adult standard.

This took the cake. Rita is, after all, married to Bob Suzuki, a first-rate neurologist, a convert, an old colleague of mine from Metro Baptist, who has been hit with more than his share of frivolous malpractice suits through the years. Was the official plan now to not only rid my son from school but to have a sanctioned Traubman V. Goldfarb parent/attorney chase after him for his computer, his go-kart, and his Israel bonds? My girls were staring in impatiently.

"Listen, Rita," I said, pounding my hands on the conference

table. "Let's resolve this right now. I'm a simple man. Tell me what to do. Should I take away his Internet? Should I have my wife drive him to the library to do his schoolwork? I want to do the right thing. We all want to do the right thing. Personally, I don't believe the right thing is being done here. Certain young people, I have a sneaking feeling, are going to walk away from these computer incidents without a scratch, while a certain friend of theirs, who apparently cares more about them than they do about him, protects them, or caves into them, or just takes the fall for them, which is worse than unfortunate, it's dishonest, and he will have to answer to me about that, being that as Jews we don't hide like cowards, or bear false witness when our friends form secret alliances against us, we stand tall and face the consequences of our actions, but even so. He graduates in three months. Then he goes to the Rutchik-Needleman School and none of you ever has to see him again. Just tell me what you think I should do."

The Hate Stops with Me gal shook her head dryly.

"You're not going to keep Eric off the Net," she said. The syllables jabbed at my kidneys. "He needs to act responsibly."

"I agree."

"And judiciously."

"I agree."

"And be punished when he doesn't. Who in this room thinks we don't have enough to do at my office tracking the activities of virulent anti-Semites and racists who would like nothing better than to spread their messages of hate, twenty-four-hours-a-day, to anyone who will listen?"

"And you do a wonderful job," Andi said to the gal. "We're grateful to you."

Eric choked back a laugh. I flicked his lip.

"Ow! Why do you have to—"

He clawed my arm; I seized his fingers and squeezed them until I heard a crunch.

"Maybe some of us in our comfortable private lives forget how serious and pressing the threats are to the safety and existence of our people," she said. "But I'm here to remind you: They're real. I fight our enemies every day. So to the three growing young men here I say, Find a good use for your computer talents. Be a tutor. Start a business. Help others. Stop seeking out ways to harm your fellow Jew."

"She's sensible," Andi whispered to me. "She is."

Mina burst in the door, out of the reach of Renata.

"We missed you," Mina sang to me, and came and sat on my lap. Suddenly I felt like a better person holding such a cute girl in my arms. Eric retracted in his seat.

"We're almost finished here."

Eric Langer, Rita said, must be held accountable for the actions the school was aware of. He would be suspended for two weeks starting Monday, to be noted on his permanent transcript. Dickie Schmertz and Lowell Simkins would not receive suspensions but were warned, along with Eric, that any further misconduct at the computer, even as passive onlookers, and they will be expelled from school.

"That's fair," Bonnie Simkins said.

Shabbat Shaloms were being exchanged and belongings collected when Andi asked Rita, "Why isn't Shoshanah Kalstein coming back to school?"

Ken Mosher ran both hands through his feathery hair; his pink youthful songleading face looked like it might just pop up with boils.

"I won't speak for Shoshanah," Rita Cohen-Suzuki said, "but we all hope she returns—she has a home here always. She knows that."

After Shabbat ended, I wasted no time disengaging Eric's computer and piling it piece by piece, wire by wire, screw-plug by screw-plug, in the center of his room. If I'd been in a different mood, I might have set the entire thing on fire, melted it, and left it for Eric to study as a kind of atonement offering, a burnt sacrifice for his dementedness. Instead, I left the computer parts stacked on the floor, wires strangling the monitor and the keyboard and the clicker, and strictly forbade him to touch them. Rather he should study their impotence. I had the Internet connection turned off in the house. I ripped down all computer-related product advertisements from above his desk. Eric should spend these two weeks, I decided, contemplating better ways to live.

To help direct him, I took out trial memberships for us at an exclusive three-story athletic club in Lime Pillars, an area twenty-five minutes east of us, with an indoor Olympic-size training pool, a six-lane running track, and a whole floor devoted to strength and conditioning. Our development community has a small workout room and spa and a pool not a few blocks away, but Eric's never liked it there and anyway I wanted us to have a place of our own to go, like the afternoons as a teenager when I would deliver refrigerators and stoves with my father, then drive over with him to his club—a card room and drinking parlor a few miles away— where we sat for an hour with his friends on a worn darkwood bench. My son was a teenager himself now—and what would we have to show for our years together?

"Nobody you know'll have to see you in trunks but me," I promised him, after I'd signed us up.

In the Talmud it says that a father is supposed to teach his son to swim. Eric knew how to kick, move his arms, and advance in water but not how to *swim*, and this bothered me, not only because of how well both my daughters swim, and how comfortable they are in the water, but because having a non-swimming son can make you feel like a personal failure. Swimming is living. Swimming is you in the world, making it. To have a son so against disrobing and plunging into a pool that he avoids pools— and lakes and oceans—what kind of future did such a son have? A change in Eric, I felt certain, would begin in the pool.

Two trips to the Ripe Pecan Whole Body Fitness Complex and I couldn't get him in. He wouldn't leave the locker room barechested. He put on flip-flops, wrapped a towel around his T-shirted shoulders, stood by a swinging door and watched me climb down into a lap lane.

I called out, "Come on, boy. New era. You'll love it."

Wouldn't come near the water's edge. Gave no reason for not coming in. Didn't seem to feel obliged to give a reason. He stood back in the new knee-low swimtrunks I'd bought him and smiled as if the occasion were something to be weathered.

On our second visit, I again called out to him in the damp, echoic, chlorinated air: "Come swim for yourself, not me."

A bathing-capped older man drew up in the lap lane next to mine, spit out a long breath, turned, and continued his slow, methodical crawl.

"Just cross the starting line," I waved. "See how you like it."

He didn't look at me doubtfully, he didn't look at me disagreeably, I don't know what you'd call his look. The facial muscles and nerve impulses did not combine to form what you'd call a traditionally denoting expression.

A couple nights later, while Eric was still suspended from school, Renata brought home word that Miss Kalstein had a disease.

"Multiple something," she said, "not dystrophy."

It turned out to be MS—and her condition was getting worse. Talk at school had started with some eighth graders, including Alison Abramson and Beth Kleinoff, the lawyers' daughters, and had spread to the lower grades. By late in the day, a few students in Renata's class had gone around saying that Miss Kalstein couldn't see right, others that she couldn't walk. One kid told everyone she was going to die, but Vashti Glick came into the classroom and said that wasn't true and not to spread false rumors. Could Miss Kalstein really die? Renata asked me. I said

I couldn't know for certain, but my guess was she'd be okay. MS is not a fatal disease, and while it can cause complications, most people adjust fairly well to it with drugs and other treatment. Renata didn't quite seem to believe me.

The next evening when I got home, speedy cartoon music and the pop-pop-pop of cartoon violence were coming from the family room, along with the sounds of little Mina dancing around the floor, mixing up in her off-key way the lyrics and melodies of "Sunrise, Sunset" and "Food Glorious Food," then adding a new couplet, "Eric loves his teacher/That's why he blinded her," which made Renata rebuke her and Eric pitch a large object against the wall that sent Mina racing out of the room, straight to my pantleg, which she clung to—hands, feet, and knees—dragging herself with me along the dining room rug and crying Eric is a monster, don't let him touch me, etc.

It occurred to me then that for the past 24 hours I had been dreaming about Shoshanah Kalstein. In my fleeting thoughts, in my most pressure-filled moments, I had been picturing her in a variety of crippled states, often in a wheelchair, joints deformed, bulging rheumy eyes calling out to me for help. It was like a series of dreams I realized I'd had many years ago about Eric's mother, Irene. In those dreams, Irene had been behind glass, and I couldn't get to her. I'd turn the doorknob, and the door wouldn't open. I'd extend an arm to her, and my hand wouldn't reach. In one moment, Irene would be pregnant and what I thought was happy in a roomy new blouse, then from another angle I'd see a gaping vacancy in her belly, a tent-flap open and no camper inside. At the time, I was in the middle of my residency, staying every third night at the hospital, up at all hours taking calls. I wanted a baby boy like nothing else. On a cot in the lounge, trying to block out all thoughts of facial trauma, I'd nod off into sleep, picturing Irene carrying my little son. Irene was a Florida girl, and I'd fallen for that—the form-fitting sheer dresses, open-toed shoes, painted toenails. She was not especially gorgeous or tall or out of my league but she had a way of making me think I'd won a prize. In those days, she had begun saying she was missing out on something. She would say she had not finished college, had not developed her own interests, and she felt *out of it*. I didn't always listen to this. When I did, I would tell her to go to college. Make something of herself. But whatever I suggested, she contradicted. She contradicted herself. To raise a family, travel, have comfortable things, be active in the Jewish community, that's what she had wanted when we met. Now it was all making her ill. I was making her ill. *Well, do better*, I would shout. *Am I a mistake?* We kept trying to have a baby. Time passed, Eric came, Irene finally did develop her own interests, which, as the court is well aware, included crafts fairs, sculpture classes, raw bars, a marginally employed non-Jew named Butler, Mateus rosé, cocaine, The Gulfside Motel in St. Augustine, the demolition derby in St. Pete, $2.49/minute calls to a telephone psychic, and the generally unstoppable following of her own star, which required, on one occasion, that she leave our twenty-one-month-old son overnight, unattended, on a docked pleasure boat in Sarasota belonging to a very wealthy restaurant owner whom she has said she does not remember ever meeting. In any case, most dreams, I have learned, are best not to remember, let alone dwell on. Better to recall that life takes its turns, character is revealed, and here I was now in my nice home, with my good second wife, my successful practice, with custody of my son, no threat of Irene, all my children safe with two reliable parents and more than enough of anything they needed, but for some reason the backs of my shoulders were crawling with sweat and dread, and I unfastened Mina from me finger by finger and went and urged Andi to call Rita Cohen-Suzuki and find out what the deal was with Shoshanah Kalstein.

Andi came back with no medical details but with the conviction that we should take Eric to visit Miss Kalstein at home. She called it "the absolute right thing to do." This way Eric could tell Miss Kalstein face-to-face he was sorry for the things he'd done, and they could both "have resolution."

"There's a reason," Andi told me in our bedroom that night, "that on Yom Kippur we go to the people we've harmed and ask their forgiveness in person. Eric can get one out of the way early this year."

I had to admit, the idea sounded very good, and not just because my long-legged wife of high character had come up with it. It sounded like just what was needed to put the school year to rest and let Eric graduate with dignity. He'd even have one up on Dickie and Lowell, who no doubt owed Shoshanah Kalstein an apology too, but whose fathers were too bull-headed ever to let it happen.

Andi arranged the visit for Sunday at 5, the day before Eric was to go back to school. Once plans were set, I made clear to Eric what Andi and I expected of him. I tutored him on what an apology consists of, stressing that the right apology could change his situation—his fate, possibly. After reviewing facial expressions and tone of voice, I practiced with him some wording options. Terms and phrases I suggested that might be useful in his situation included *I made a bad error in judgment*; *I apologize for what I've done*; *it was never my intention to hurt you or anyone by my actions*; *I made an immature decision*; *I've learned from my mistakes*; *I'd like to ask your forgiveness, please*; and *typical of my age, I guess you'd say*. Bringing up his teacher's multiple sclerosis, I said, would be insensitive, but it would be okay to ask how she's feeling in general. Eric said he'd say anything to Miss Kalstein that I asked him to.

I said, "Even, 'Would you please go in and model that satin nightgown on the back of your bedroom door for me, *gveret*? It would bring me pleasure.'"

He indicated that he would.

I told him I was joking and that he should be able to tell a joke from what's serious.

His eyes noted the distinction. It made me believe he was capable of grasping how offensive his behavior in the last couple months had been.

I laid my hand on his clicker, which sat atop his stack of computer parts and cables like a mini plastic head on an awkwardly constructed statue at the center of his floor.

"Keep studying this impotent piece of machinery," I said. "Study it and imagine yourself successful—and strong. Not at computers. But at something real, involving a real living future on Earth."

He agreed that he would.

I asked would he go in swimming on our next trip to the club.

He nodded yes.

"You're not mocking me?" I said. "Agreeing with everything I say?"

He said that he wasn't.

Shoshanah Kalstein lived on a narrow, winding street two blocks up from a busy through-way in our city's popular Centerbridge area. I ordinarily have no reason to visit Centerbridge, which I guess you'd characterize as a bohemian area—a lot of artists, single adult people, men walking their strange dog breed types, young childless couples, kids out of college, interracial groupings, and so forth. A high uninsured area. I get very few referrals from Centerbridge. It used to be one of the older money areas of town. There's a big park where they stage pop music concerts during the summer. In the front windows of some of the divided Reconstruction-era houses across from the park, residents hang flags whose symbolism is lost on me. I would not consider Centerbridge inviting to outsiders, but people seem to like it.

Miss Kalstein lived in a duplex, with vines that climbed the left side of a single wide gable. Big thick bushes ran along either side of the property. The front yard was densely planted. The whole place looked like it was about to flower.

Eric and Andi and I parked along the curb and rehearsed once more the key elements of his apology. Eric was wearing a button-down collared shirt a bit too short at the wrist, and a snug vest. He had on a dash of eau d'cologne and his hair was brushed. His jacket was folded in his lap. He seemed touched by the whole undertaking. But with kids of today—and with Eric, too—you have a hard time knowing what's sincere, so I reminded him to *show* Miss Kalstein he meant everything he said.

"Don't ever let her think you're talking out your blowhole."

Andi gave us both a proud, encouraging pucker of the chin.

As we walked up the drive, I could feel spring at our heels. We'd been having unseasonably icy dawns as late as this past week and it was time for all that to be over. Miss Kalstein let us in. She had on a beaded outfit with matching drawstring bottoms and was standing in front of a galvanized tin bucket filled with cut witch hazel branches: the strange orange horn-blossoms were uncurled in their miraculous little theaters of life. We crowded into the living room. The first surprise, of course, was Mosher, sitting in the wing-back chair. I realized I shouldn't be surprised to see Mosher and in the best seat. Shoshanah Kalstein probably wanted a security presence, and who could blame her. His guitar case was at his small feet. She opened the front curtains all the way. The gentle waves of late-afternoon light made it feel like we were at a higher elevation. There were Jewish National Fund posters on the two full walls—one of a green mountain forest in the Galilee lit by a shaft of sunlight, the other of boys and girls planting trees on a hill alongside their parents and grandparents. Andi and Shoshanah stood together by that one.

"Your home smells great," Andi said.

"Ken made a Turkish salad," Shoshanah Kalstein said. "That's roasted peppers you smell."

The woman appeared to be in fine health. Andi talked with her about cooking and food-shopping and an outreach program she is involved in that helps feed low-income children.

Eric sat himself in the far corner, on a low bean-filled seat shaped like the fat top of a thumb.

"Come on up," I said, taking a folding chair. "Closer."

I pulled him and myself next to Ken Mosher. Mosher didn't seem anxious or angry. He seemed happy, lucky to be this close to Shoshanah Kalstein on a Sunday, and closer in age to Eric than to me.

"So, guitar's your thing," I said to Mosher. I saw him evaluating the extent of my hair loss. "I've got a daughter who plays the viola."

"Sure, Renata," Mosher said, flipping out his hair a little. "Great kid."

"You know my girls? You know my little Mina, too? Sings and dances? Second grade? Cute as a button."

Mosher claimed not to know her, though he had seen her at least as recently as the Conference of Remedial Alternatives.

"You will," I said. "She's going to be something. Real personal magnetism, like you."

Shoshanah Kalstein began to appear uncomfortable. She and Mosher started doing a little thing with their eyes.

"Should we give out roles?" I said.

Nobody seemed to know what I meant by this. Miss Kalstein moved behind the wing of Mosher's chair. Unstabilized autoimmune inflammatory condition or not, this was a well-put-together woman, but Andi, I couldn't help noticing, had a good two inches on her and didn't give up anything in the chest. I was suddenly proud of my wife's appearance. She does pretty damned all right for a mother of two-slash-three past forty. Miss Kalstein had a distant sadness in her eyes. Eric hadn't said a word yet. The room was losing its sun.

"Eric appreciates that you'd have us over," Andi said to Shoshanah Kalstein. Eric turned bright red. He shifted from side to side on his ungainly buttocks.

"It's true," Eric mumbled, almost inaudibly. "We appreciate it."

"You appreciate it," I said.

"Okay," he snapped.

"Don't snap," I said. "*You* appreciate it."

Shoshanah Kalstein set her fingers on the back of Ken Mosher's chair, very near his shoulders. I had the impression, much like at Meet the Parents in the Sukkah Night, and even more so, that this woman wanted motherhood.

Eric's eyes were lowered.

"The flowering branches?" he said cautiously, motioning toward the door.

"It's witch hazel," said Shoshanah Kalstein cheerfully.

"Sure it is," I said.

"They started opening again just this week," she continued, using her hands.

"Haven't we shown him witch hazel along the river?" I asked Andi. "I know Renata can identify witch hazel. She'd know witch hazel eyes-closed, by smell."

"We had a lot of it behind our yard growing up," Shoshanah Kalstein said to Eric. "It's one of the little things about home you miss when you live far away."

By the wide front window hung two brass cups and a brass bowl. Miss Kalstein told us where in Israel these had come from. She offered up a few sentences about her years living on a moshav, working on an egg farm and a flower farm and for the forestry service, then she looked as if she had given us more of something than she'd intended.

I waited. Andi waited. I could have popped Eric on the back of the head. Couldn't he see this was his moment to step in? She was part-vulnerable.

Andi asked Miss Kalstein if they could speak in the kitchen. The women closed the door to us. In a few minutes, the door half-opened and Andi waved over Eric and then the door swallowed him too. This left me beside Ken Mosher.

I had no desire to engage this young man in conversation,

and I imagined the feeling was mutual. Mosher put on a folk music record. It did smell like something good was cooking behind the kitchen door—eggplants? potatoes?

A second song came on. I decided to tactfully raise the subject of Miss Kalstein's health. I said I didn't wish to poke my head in where it didn't belong but I was a medical doctor and I wondered who her neurologist was. I may know the guy, I said.

"Suzuki," he answered, as if any half-wit at school or synagogue would know this.

"Holy Christ," I blurted out. Was there a conspiracy, even among people I'd known for years, to keep information from me about Shoshanah Kalstein's true state of health? Adjusting my voice, I said, "He's first rate. She'll get the best care available."

Mosher went on tapping his foot to the folk music record.

"In terms of her...actual condition," I asked, "are things...stabilizing?"

"She's good. She's a tough lady," he said. "You'd be surprised based on how nice she is."

"I wouldn't be surprised at all," I said. "She seems both the tough and the nice type."

"She doesn't want anybody feeling sorry for her," he said. "She just wants to be left to live her life, like anybody else."

Catching his drift, I said, "I want you to know, I keep Eric off the computer now. One hundred percent completely. He's on a short leash. Last month's...incident...with her and you...was the last time. Whatever part he played or didn't play—was the last time under my roof. I just wanted you to hear that from my mouth. She has zero to worry about from the Langer household."

Mosher nodded.

He picked up a section of the Sunday paper. He offered me a section, then put on eyeglasses and began reading. Another song came on. I gave the fellow credit: not even married, he was sticking with a woman whose disease could permanently disable her without warning. Motor function. Whole nervous system.

A tambourine came into the song.

"You've got a lot going for you," I said to Mosher. The eyeglasses made him look wiser. "My kids don't realize how fortunate they are. So much of everything. The expectations are all screwy now."

He continued reading.

"But they'll learn. At public school my son would get torn up joint from joint. I'd have to cancel patients to personally reconstruct his face."

"I wouldn't know about that," Mosher said. "I don't know your son."

"Who does?" I said.

Mosher looked through the arts section of the paper. He circled something with a pencil. The women and Eric were behind the kitchen door a long while.

At last Andi and Shoshanah Kalstein came out. There was a contentment on their faces that was almost foreign. It was like two leaders emerging from a successful summit meeting, who had inhabited some shared and lofty territory that you could not inhabit. Eric was not with them.

"I hope you're not leaving my son alone in your kitchen with all that delicious-smelling food," I said to Shoshanah Kalstein.

The women's faces looked clean and frank and unperturbed and guileless. It was very pleasant then to be in Shoshanah Kalstein's home at dusk, with contented smiles, and the Jewish National Fund posters on the walls—and given the history of this school year, it felt like a stroke of good luck. Maybe Miss Kalstein would suddenly surprise us and say that she and Ken had been making this big meal for us too and we would all sit together and break pita and eat eggplant and potatoes and Turkish salad. The more I looked at these two women, the more optimistic I was getting. A bright future is what I think we all want for each other.

When Eric entered from the kitchen, I saw that he had honored me. Whatever he had said to Miss Kalstein had been accepted, was enough. He smelled like the kitchen and the flowers and the cologne and himself. He was now silent again and pleased and he ruminated upon something that seemed mysterious and unthreatening. I put my arm around his waist and held him. We were thanked. We were walked to the door. Andi and Shoshanah Kalstein shook hands.

Riding home, with a Hebrew/English folk music CD of Andi's on the stereo, I breathed and stretched my muscles with an almost childlike sense of optimism. I quit wondering if a conspiracy of silence raged against me. Instead, I grew confident that Shoshanah Kalstein's condition would stabilize, if it hadn't already, and that when she was ready she would return triumphantly to Traubman V. Goldfarb and live several more decades in good health, as free of attacks and symptoms as medicine would allow. I pictured her bringing a class of eighth graders into an assembly where Ken Mosher walked back and forth across a stage, guitar strapped to his shoulder, clapping and strumming and leading them in "Not By Might, Not By Power" and "Sissu et Yerushalayim."

I had similar optimism about Eric. From what he and Andi described, he had made a bridge between himself and another person—a woman—that boded well to me. He had not run from responsibility, and had ended up acting bravely. In his own way I knew Eric cared for Miss Kalstein, and it sounded as though he had communicated this to her in a non-destructive, non-alienating fashion, even using two phrases we had practiced together: *I made an error in judgment. I apologize for my actions.* It was this optimism, then, and pride in my only son, that caused me to say yes when, in his room, he asked if he could plug back in his computer and reconnect to the Internet. He wanted to check e-mail. Who are you expecting e-mail from? I asked. He did not answer. I was not suspicious. We were standing equidistant from the statue of his inert components, he by the bedside, I by the desk. The little white satin man near the ceiling whose knees hang over the crescent moon looked protectively happy. Eric's expression seemed to suggest that he'd learned something. An innocence in him showed. Even now, I don't blame myself for saying yes. Perhaps only fathers who have had trouble raising their sons will understand when I say I thought I was helping him build more bridges.

He went back to school the next day, which would have been Monday, March 19. I was very busy at the office that week and got called into the hospital more than once. I was rarely home before 9 p.m. I had just enough time to take quick status reports from Andi and the kids and catch a bite of dinner. I was back in at 6:30 a.m. That week I saw two new patients—both under twenty—who had speech problems resulting from irregularities in jaw growth. It's one thing to have difficulty speaking. It's another to not have the complete bodily apparatus for speech available. But we take care of them. Shoot X-rays, start models. What gets me is imagining how some of these young people suffer before coming in for treatment at all. I did a chin that week and a mandibular bone graft for a guy in his mid-twenties who, the first time he came into the office, told me without a shred of self-pity that no woman had ever looked at him with love. It's then that I'm a repairman, my father's son, giving what I have to my patients. So I was busy and exhausted that week but optimistic.

I am quite sure that the Internet service was not brought back on in the house until Wednesday, March 21, the first official day of spring. I wasn't around to check on Eric, but even if I had been, history would suggest that I don't know for long what's really going on in his head, no matter how closely I involve myself in his life. That Shabbos, I recall, was peaceful. I napped after shul in the warm sunlight. Eric read, Renata and Mina played at the homes of synagogue friends. We don't use TV and computers on Shabbat, and each week the children find good ways, as their ancestors have done for thousands of years, to occupy themselves and sanctify the day. At about three o'clock, Eric and I sat at the breakfast table and ate challah and butter in tranquility.

The next morning, Sunday, Eric called me into his room. The computer was on: one of his animated outer-space military screen scenes. Eric's face was impassable, a face I thought we had put behind us.

"What if I told you something," he said. "Would you believe me?"

"That depends if it was true," I said.

"If I tell you, it's true," he said.

"That's your first untruth right there," I said. He swiveled away from me in his computer chair. "Have you not kept the truth from me plenty of times through the years?"

"All right, now you can get out of here," he said.

"But this time I'll believe you," I said, tousling his hair. I thought we had an accord.

"No, this time get out of here."

"They welcomed you back to school this week like one of the group, didn't they, boy?"

No answer.

"They didn't realize how much they would miss you but they did, didn't they? The girls too, I mean."

A slight grinding of teeth.

"You're a good kid," I said.

I wanted to kiss him. He pointed to the door.

I went and asked Renata if something was eating Eric. She didn't know. Andi didn't know. I assumed because it was a Sunday, it wasn't about school. I'd had a long week and I didn't give it a lot of thought.

"The Doom Dokkter Attack," as it is now called by everyone, including the 75,000 readers of the *Greater Southeast Jewish Report*, which has covered it in bold-stroke detail for the past two weeks, occurred Monday night, March 26. To recount the entire sequence of events—starting with Vashti Glick's discovery Tuesday at 7:30 a.m. of an "anti-Semitic cyber-terrorist attack against the school and possibly other Metro Jewish entities"; the 11 a.m. decision to shut down the computer systems at all Jewish schools in the city as well as at numerous charitable and religious institutions; the quick and mistaken blaming of a small Aryan Brotherhood group based fifty miles south of here; and on and on, leading to the Wednesday identification, Thursday interrogation, and Friday expulsion of Eric—would stretch my patience past the limit.

And yet somehow I have managed to keep relatively calm throughout most of this last stage of Eric's Traubman V. Goldfarb ordeal. I don't know how this has happened. You would have thought that on that Wednesday evening, after Eric took credit for the computer attack and thought he was a very clever fellow and told his sisters and neighbors how funny it was that he had panicked the school and the girls and the local Jewish community and how easy it had been to do, that I would have picked him up by his fat arms and slammed him around and slammed his computer into his desk and possibly even called my family members, including my extremely decent wife, words that should not be spoken much less repeated. And it is true that at times that evening I literally wanted to choke the living voice out of Eric, shame him, crush each of his chubby hands, knuckle by knuckle, metacarpal by metacarpal, and prevent him from raining down one more drop of trouble on this house via his dark wizardry at the computer. It is also true that there were moments I could not keep my hands to themselves, when I shoved Eric against the hanging *Where Are You? What Time Will You Be Back?* board on our kitchen wall, for example, harder than I meant to, snapping his head back, the skull thudding against the board, half a dozen pink Post-It notes sent flying across his shoulders. But such episodes were brief. I did not deal any blows I would regret.

Instead, in the dining room, with all of my household gathered round, my toes digging into the thick Sephardic rug that Lazaro Schmertz the importer got me a great deal on five years ago, I asked Eric calmly, perhaps feeling even a little wounded, what possibly could have motivated him to post the following flashing message (supplied by Renata) on every computer screen at school:

Protecters and perpetraiters
NOW YOU GO DOWN.

Doom Dokkter's comin for
YOUR
AZZ
!!!

We looked at the words as a family.

"It's a little sick, isn't it?"

"They know what they do," Eric said.

"What do they do?" little Mina asked.

"They," and then Eric muttered something that made it sound as if his entire mouth cavity was filled with teeth.

"Speak slowly," Andi said.

"They don't give an S," Renata translated.

"Is that an answer?" I said.

Eric's lips pinched thin and slightly purple and raw with conviction.

"Somebody showed them what they needed to get shown," he said.

"What did you show *them*?" asked Andi. It was the first time I had ever seen my wife struggle to place hope in this child of my first marriage. "That you can get expelled from school? And lose the respect of your people? And possibly have a crime now on your permanent legal record?"

Mina cackled.

"You're going down, Eric," she said. "Down to the ground."

Renata made a gizzard-squeezing gesture toward her younger sister.

"What did your message *mean*, boy?" I asked.

"If they want to have their school, they can have it," Eric said, his voice making an angry, hidden circle.

The first part of Eric's Conference of Involuntary Removal from Day School that Friday was open to anyone who, in Vashti Glick's words, "had been affected by Tuesday's computer-related incidents and wanted the opportunity to voice their feelings and concerns." Nearly forty people jammed into the meeting room. More waited in the office, staring in through the narrow bars of glass. The blue-framed proverbs, gifts from the fourth grade, had all been taken down. The walls were empty, the white dry-erase board smudged clean. Parents seated around the U-shaped tables shared armrests with friends. Daughters peered past mothers who leaned over grandmothers' shoulders. A line of teenagers crowded the walls. The smallest children sat in the center. Cantor Lichler and Shira were there. Rhondalee Abramson and Alison were there. Dickie Schmertz and Lowell Simkins. Teachers, administrators. The room was so packed, I could feel the warm breath of the Judaic studies curriculum coordinator on my cheek. It was just a couple weeks past Purim, and references to the Book of Esther—to Haman being impaled on his own stake, to all the Jews of the kingdom being saved from extermination thanks to the courage of Mordecai and Esther—could be heard on all sides of me.

Eric and I sat, shoulder to shoulder, where we had at the previous Conference of Remedial Alternatives. This time, however, Andi was absent. The night before, she had stayed up late, lecturing me in language I couldn't have imagined from her before—for instance, that "Eric might truly be losing his grip" and what was I going to do about it?—stopping herself just short of demanding that I get him outside professional help. I watched her pace anxiously in front of the provincial French armoire and five-drawer chest I bought her for her birthday the year we married, waiting for when she would come into bed and soften like she does, slide closer and believe in me. Outside in the half-moonlight, at the edge of our woods, an unmated mockingbird kept bursting into his spring triplicate appeals of song. By the time Andi fell asleep, without saying goodnight, she had vowed to steer clear of today's meeting and to keep the girls out of school besides.

When the meeting began and the voices rose, and the stones began to fly from every corner of the room and at once, I was surprised only to find that they were being directed almost exclusively at *me*. How had *I* let this happen? What was *I* doing that my son is so filled with *hate*? Am I not *involved* in his *activities*? This is not *the first time*, Doctor, which makes the matter *particularly* troubling. How about if you taught him instead to be a *light* unto the nations? Given all we have to fear, and all the problems of this world, with all our history, and the situation in Israel, is *this* what we need from our children? You're not a dummy. You knew the score. I feel sorry for you, Kip, I really do. These actions are a threat to our very...

I was quiet in a way I had not been in a very long time. Tempted as I would have been on another occasion to slice my accusers up the center and pin them to the table with examples of their own hypocrisy and failures, I love my people, and I found myself unable to stop wondering, silently, and during my quiet replies, how in the world my son—whatever he stored in his dark basement of grievances—could want to send hundreds of matching little notes to his fellow Jews saying they were going to be destroyed. Had I played a role in that? For his part, Eric seemed to be seated in a kind of glass booth, sneaking looks around, some boastful, some contemptuous, some suspicious, some defeated, but mostly he seemed to be concentrating on ideas he'd picked up in places I knew nothing of. At one point a fifth grader seeking praise stood forward and asked, "Do adults here know how much hate writing there is on the Internet?" and offered to lead them to it. A bustle ensued. Cantor Lichler, with his vivid and neatly trimmed red sideburns and gorgeously embroidered Bukharan kippah, revealed that a congregant had showed him something on the Internet yesterday where "The Jews" were blamed for directing "the current genocide against white Christians in America." It had made him physically sick. Do we want to toss fuel, he boomed, on the very fires that we're trying to put out? It's a sad day, an older lady said. Who's Doom Dokkter? a second grader on the floor wanted to know.

When things got more personal, when Rhondalee Abramson, for instance, perfectly tanned and with a queen's threading of gold in her hair, raised a hand to her forehead as if there were a glare in the building and talked about the "mental suffering unleashed on Alison by that truly—disturbing—overfed—individual—who, I'm sorry but, I can't even bring myself to look at," I indicated with an eyebrow to Rita Cohen-Suzuki that I had had it with this portion of the program. Rhondalee Abramson didn't stop, however, until everyone in the room saw that she had gotten her fill. Then a second lawyer's wife took over. From there, Devi Kreuzer, snazzy in a ponytail, legs crossed tight, pulling at the shoulders of her blouse after every other sentence, dug in, testifying about "not being able to feel even close to one hundred percent safe" in her own school this year and not wanting to *know* the damage that had been permanently done to her. Eventually, after the last looks in the room had been given, the last hand shaken, the last wave exchanged, when no one could be heard behind thick pink lipstick to be saying, "It's a *shandeh*, a disgrace," and "One less thing to worry about," I found myself alone with Eric, Rita, Vashti Glick, Janet Greenberg, and with Eric's math and sciences teacher Reuvain Pfefferbaum, a bristly, slender man with long features who gave the impression that he was generally sympathetic to my son.

The atmosphere was one in which a profound failure could be felt to have occurred, though I don't know that any of us would have agreed what that failure was. Sheets of blank paper lay scattered. On the floor, one sheet was partly crumpled where children had been playing a game of "Hangman." Under a table, some girls had left behind one of those Truth Detectors made from folded paper, where you manipulate the base one way and the next, then open up a petal and receive the answer to your question: *Definitely Not. I'd Say So.* Everywhere in the room gave the smell of women— of women's hands, women's clothes, of women forbearing, women running the show. I think we all tried to put a good face on things, even Vashti Glick, who to her credit did not gloat, but since the outcome of the meeting had already been determined, nearly everything that was said came out sounding lifeless. Reuvain Pfefferbaum did emphasize that he held a lot of hope for Eric, urging him to learn a kind of math I was not familiar with. Janet Greenberg offered a carefully worded message of encouragement. Rita Cohen-Suzuki wrote down some procedural things, handed me a couple forms to sign, then stood on her platform heels and broke into a cheerful story about a bright boy she knew growing up who was expelled from his yeshiva after committing some regrettable actions but who eventually went on to become very successful on Wall Street, have a big family, and make a huge financial contribution to the school years later, plus be a great supporter of Israel.

Eric asked what regrettable actions he had committed. "That's not the part of the story I choose to remember," Rita answered, rocking on her heels and winking at him in her matching skirt and neckerchief, which was ornamented with the dove-and-olive-branch stickpin. "And I hope you'll turn out to be the same way."

On our walk to the parking lot, we ran into Dickie Schmertz and Lowell Simkins, who were waiting for Dickie's mom to pick them up. The boys looked a little embarrassed. Dickie's eyebrows formed an exaggerated expression of tension.

"Hey, Dr. Langer?" he said.

Lowell Simkins said something to Eric in a private language of theirs. I didn't trust these boys any more, but it disturbed me that this could be the end of Eric's friendships with them.

"Keep in touch now with Eric, guys," I said. "You know where to find him. A friendship like the three of you have is something you hold onto for life."

A young teacher joyfully holding his tiny newborn walked past us toward the blossoming spring sky with his wife and a second young man. At his car the teacher lifted the baby high and laughed and said to his friend, "Three weeks ago she knew the entire Torah by heart!" and the friend laughed and said, "This may sound funny, but at times I feel I've known her forever!"

Faye Schmertz drove up with her dog and idled in the pick-up lane. Her headlights were on and they didn't need to be. Dickie and Lowell got in back, and Eric and I stood at the passenger's window while the boys leaned forward and played with the dog.

"Eric, I heard," Faye said. Her tone made it sound as if she was telling Eric he had died.

"We want you to come over to our house anytime you like and play with Dickie. You're still part of our family."

From the back seat Dickie nodded at his mother's words, while scratching the dog.

I could see Eric was ready to take off. I pulled him close to me.

"Listen, Faye. This guy right here's going to have some privileges taken away for a period of time and he's going to get his act together, he's going to figure out what's real and what's make-believe, and then listen. He's going to call your guy up, and they're going to play together with the other one back there and keep the friendship cooking." I clapped Eric's shoulder. "Because this guy's on the ball. Just like those two. There's nothing those two have that this one doesn't. All right? And that goes for the other boys at this school. The good-looking ones too, I'm talking about. The studs. The Brent Westenthals of the world. You know what I mean."

"We'll barbecue," said Faye, with a promissary expression, and then she scratched the dog. "We'll see you after Pesach?"

Eric raised a thumb to Faye Schmertz and whispered in my ear, "Can we please cut the insane adult chatter now? You're making my brain need to explode in tiny pieces on the sidewalk."

"After Pesach, it is," I said to Faye and the boys, and raised a matching thumb.

That week it came from all angles at the house. First, The Hate Stops with Me gal, joined by Lou Fine, the city's unofficial anti-intolerance czar, came to interview Eric about the "Doom Dokkter Attack." Eric sat in flip-flops and soccer shorts on the expensive couch and watched them try to crack his nut, offering them the same answers he had offered Andi and me and the administrators, namely that "they" didn't give an S, that "they" can have the school, that "they" had gotten theirs. After a short while, Lou Fine and the Hate Stops with Me gal declared that Eric was "a lot simpler than meets the eye." He was not hiding any real story, they said, because he didn't have a real story to hide. They accused him of being an aggressive spoiled-rich suburban punk kid who liked making trouble because it was fun, because it made him feel powerful, who thought there was no blowback to anything, who believed you could terrify a nice, patient, tolerant, liberal-minded group of Jewish school people and they would keep coddling and nurturing and forgiving you. But now he was being watched. Now his every move was being watched. Know, Eric, that you're already on our "Metro Haters to Watch" list and you're on your way to making the Southeast "100 Online Haters Beware." If it's attention and publicity you want, we'll give you more than you bargained for. We'll jam attention down your throat and see how you like that. We will not be intimidated. We will see *who goes down*.

"I don't want publicity."

"What *do* you want, Eric Langer?"

Eric gave no answer. They left as furious as when they arrived.

I continued to believe that my son had not "attacked" the Day School just for kicks. Even if he had perhaps wanted to make himself into some kind of bigshot. We had just been building bridges! He had delicately sniffed Shoshanah Kalstein's witch hazel branches just the week before!

The next night, a parent-friend of Andi's and mine came by with word that a newly fortified brigade of Traubman V. Goldfarb parent/attorneys was putting together a civil liability suit not against Eric but against *me*, for *negligence*, i.e., for not taking reasonable steps to prevent my minor child with a known propensity for hacking from breaking into the school's computer system and issuing harmful threats. The plan, in other words, was: Sue Dr. Moneybags, The Surgeon, The Can't-be-blamed-often-enough-in-this-society Father. Link him to every occurrence of rash, fever, asthma, vomiting, diarrhea, nosebleed, sinus infection, ear infection, allergy attack, dislocated wrist, chronic fatigue syndrome, hyperactivity, hypertension, sleep disorder, and mood imbalance exhibited by a schoolchild or other community member since the Doom Dokkter Attack, as well as to the sudden worsening of Shoshanah Kalstein's condition. Miss Kalstein, we learned, had spent a night in the hospital this weekend after experiencing an unfamiliar shock sensation in the back of the leg. The parent/attorneys intended to show that Eric's repeated hacking, his history of reckless messaging were the "actual and proximate cause" of her latest injuries.

It kept going. A black Department of Justice official named Chalmers Chenier stopped by to "have a little talk with Eric" about what he had done on the computer to the Traubman V. Goldfarb Day School Academy. Mr. Chenier wore a suit. He had a calm and unflappable demeanor. His shoes were a well-polished cordovan and his socks were violet with a stripe of tiny silver diamonds. This was the one visit that shook Eric up. Pesach was approaching, Andi and the girls were starting to get rid of chumetz, and one or more of them kept bringing out non-kosher-for-Pesach treats to offer Mr. Chenier. This was top stuff: biscotti, shortbread, tropical-flavor gourmet frozen juice sticks. We were really laying it on the guy. We needed to. The man was not happy with what he knew.

"So to you this was an innocent schoolboy prank?" he asked Eric with a slow interrogative drawl. A voice like his is not commonly heard in our living room. I could see Eric sweat at the hairline as he offered his usual elliptical answers. Chenier wasn't buying them. Who were these "they" figures? Specific targets? Students? A teacher or teachers? Other individuals involved at any level with the Traubman V. Goldfarb Day School Academy? Eric's mouth sealed tight. He bobbed his head about and lifted his eyebrows as if he might answer, but in the end he gave no answer. I wondered if there was an answer. Chenier asked Eric if he regarded his actions as a crime and if so, what kind of crime. Mina and Renata and Andi were by then watching from the dining room, Andi holding a silver tray of goodies, ready to bring them in with a fresh pot of chamomile tea. Chenier didn't say much else. He didn't have to. He gave Eric his card, wrote down the addresses of two government websites, and told Eric to e-mail him after he'd figured out whether he had committed a crime and, if so, what the penalty could be if prosecuted.

Eric said, "You'll have to talk to my dad. He dragged my computer through an oil pool in the garage, then kicked it against the wall. It might be destroyed."

"Snail mail is acceptable," Chenier said to Eric.

Before he left, I asked Mr. Chenier, who was about my age, what he thought of Preston (Chip) Dexter Junior High as a school for Eric. Based on what he'd seen of Eric this evening, would that school help my son get his act together, or would it just turn him for the worse? You hear so much bad stuff about the public schools, I said. Chenier didn't know the first thing about Chip Dexter.

"He'll get his act together," he said. "He's got no choice but to."

After Mr. Chenier's visit, I took half a day off work to enroll Eric in Preston (Chip) Dexter Junior High. I had been hearing that the place had a good reputation for a public school. Still, something in me did not want my son going there. Part of why I work so hard is to give my children the best education possible. My father would have taken me out of public school in a heartbeat, he always said, if he could have afforded to. Eric wasn't the least bit worried about going to Chip Dexter, and since I had no better plan for him, there we were, pulling off Powers Ferry Road, not far from the JCC, curling down and around onto the asphalt. We parked near the cluster of white buildings that look from the road like a hideous modern art complex or else a state correctional facility, huge concrete cylinders and cubes pressed against each other, where every angle of rooftop looks like it would make a nice perch for a sharpshooter. Who, except a couple girls at my office, sent their children to public school?

"This isn't exactly going to be the Rutchik-Needleman School," I said to Eric as we got our temporary badges from the armed security guard. "If you decide you want to go to a secular private school, even if it's an hour away, I'll..."

A smiling bald guidance counselor with a rim of slick hair, Mr. Nagler, came out to greet us. He smelled of herbal lotion, displayed receding gum tissue, and had traces of gravy stains to the right and left of his tie. He quickly showed himself to be a gracious and effective bureaucrat and I couldn't help but place the first bit of trust in him. In his office, he assured Eric and me that Chip Dexter was one of the top-rated junior highs academically in the county, a three-time-consecutive state gold medal "We Achieve Higher" school, and that Eric would be a welcome presence here. I decided to skip telling him about Eric's expulsion. He would learn what he needed to when the transcript arrived.

"There won't be any problems here with Eric being an observant Jew, will there?" I said.

Heavens no, said the counselor. Chip Dexter was a hate-free zone. He pointed to a yellow poster over one of the secretaries' heads that said as much.

"So no penalties by his teachers for taking off Jewish holidays or not participating in extracurricular things on the Sabbath?"

Nagler said no.

"Well, if that's so," I said, "it'll be a welcome change from my public school days. I once had to fatten Eddie Frontier's lip in seventh grade for not shutting up on the basketball court about 'Don't let Little Kip the Yiddie shoot. Shut him down, shut him down,' and then surrounding me with elbows and kicks to the shin. I laid one right in the top of his mouth. His buddies demolished me afterward, but I didn't care. Eddie thought twice from then on."

"I'm sorry you had that experience," said the counselor. "Surely we live in different times. We all deserve the chance to grow, wouldn't you agree?" He started a file on Eric. "Langer/Nagler," he said with a crisp grin. "An anagram."

Eric looked through the list of classes.

"You don't offer Hebrew as a foreign language, I suppose," I said to Nagler.

"Wish we did," he said. "Spanish, French, Italian, German, and starting two years ago Japanese. The parents wanted to make sure our kids could get a head start in international business, if they so chose. Of course, to me, the darned computers are a foreign language in and of themselves."

Eric chose Shop and Italian 1 for his electives.

"Italian?" I said with a good laugh. "Actually, I can explain that decision to you, Mr. Nagler, in two words: Meet girls."

Eric would start the following Monday, after *yontov*. Depending on how his transcript looked, he might have to take summer school to be promoted with his class. Eric didn't seem to mind. In fact, he was unflinchingly curious during our entire visit with the counselor. Touring the halls, I saw nothing but an endless crowded geometry of walls, against which any group of rough, brawny *goyim* could potentially hold my son by the shoulders and loosen his front teeth for not wishing to join the Young Republicans Club or be saved by Jesus Christ. Eric did not see things this way. He stared with fascination as hoodlum-looking characters sauntered along in big clothes, bobbing to earphones. He watched the fresh local peaches with tight middles in denim stroll two by two. His face expressed possibilities.

"I don't mind this place at all," he said on our way to the car.

Back at home Eric answered a phone call on our house line from an elderly man who had read about him in the *Greater Southeast Jewish Report*. We were getting no fewer than five calls like this per day. I had told Eric he could hang up on these people but he never did. The man had called to say, in heavily accented English, "Shame on you, young man. Learn who you are. You hear me? Learn what your people have been through. Then you won't act like such a fool." "Thanks, Grandpa," Eric had said, near a whisper, not belligerently, choking on his own breath. He looked sad and confused after these calls, like he was crammed into an uninhabitable cell with no chance of transfer. Not having a computer in his room was cramping his lifestyle, I know. It made him twitchy like an obsessive. He and Mina nearly tore each other limb from limb one afternoon, when she came home and found him straddling her sparkly little painted desk chair, using her computer. "HIS FINGERS ARE TOUCHING MY KEYPAD!" she screamed, then rushed at him with her head like a horn and tried to gash his side with the sharp edges of her barrettes.

The days were staying light now till after seven. Trees and bushes along the river were in bloom. I got home and could walk out to the edge of the woods and watch the changing light on the backs of lizards and see the tiny flowers that colored the wet floor and listen to birds sing to each other while other birds flipped around in the high branches, recreating. I missed my dad most at those times. We had Seder at Andi's brother's. That night in the bedroom, Andi kept her distance from me, as she had all week. In our few minutes together she looked at me (not for the first time in our marriage but in a more immediately recognizable way) like I might not be the man she had chosen years ago to trust. I pretended I wasn't bothered. A couple days later, Eric called his mother in South Florida without telling me. She invited him to spend two weeks with her this summer.

"I could go to the beach every day," he told me.

"You don't even swim," I said.

"There's things to see at a beach."

"You're telling me you'd put your fat rolls on display every day for those South Florida beach bunnies?"

"I might."

"Bring money," I told him. "Those girls down there are expensive. You might want to take out heartbreak insurance."

No answer.

"So what did you tell her?"

"Yes."

"That you'd go?"

"What did I just say?"

"I'm for it," I said. "If that's what you want for two weeks. It's only two weeks. Some good might come of it. Is she working? Who's going to watch you?"

"She'll watch me."

"I just hope when the day comes, she remembers that she made a commitment to you. That's all I'm saying. That she shows up at the airport and has something for you to do during the day. And that you come home the minute you're supposed to. Needless to say, I assume she expects *me* to buy you the plane ticket."

The day before Eric was to start public school, Renata and Andi took him to the mall to pick out a new outfit. They came back with four full bags of clothing. Renata told me that Eric had called himself "The Overweight Lover" as he tried things on, grinning, in the department store.

I could feel that something was changing in my house that I didn't understand, and I called everyone into the family room. Mina snuggled against my leg. Andi said, "Can you believe how beautifully Renata sang at Seder? I can't believe her pitch," and I said, "That child has music talent that comes from who-knows-where. My only talent is fixing bones."

"Please don't talk about my voice or my talent," Renata said, entering.

"What about *my* talent?" Mina asked.

"You've got so much cuteness talent," I said, plucking her chin, "the milkman must have delivered it all."

"*Look, look,*" Mina pointed at the doorway. In walked Eric wearing a new untucked periwinkle short-sleeve collared shirt, khakis, clean white sneakers, and a flat white cap with a periwinkle stripe. This looked to me like a black style.

"Tell him he looks good, Dad," Renata said. She was reclining next to Andi, under the big straw Chinese hat.

I had never known Eric to show that he cared how he looked.

He slouched with his back to the Israeli-tiled mirror, not really looking at anyone.

"You mean, tell Casanova he's the man?" I said.

"I think he looks great," Andi said. "The blue flatters him."

"We helped him pick it out," Renata said.

"He looks like a doof," Mina said, and giggled.

Renata made Mina flinch. I thought Eric looked a doof myself.

"Was your purpose all along to get kicked out of Traubman V. Goldfarb?" I asked.

He eyed me sharply, then glanced at Andi and his sisters. It was like he was trying to step into some other idea of being my son.

"Cat got your tongue?" I said.

Eric stood up straight, manly.

"Say it," I said.

"If you want me to show you something, I'll show you," he said. "But don't act now like you cared, because you didn't care."

I leaped up.

"Don't *ever* accuse me of not caring about you, boy," I shouted, backing him against the Israeli-tiled mirror. Above his Adam's apple a single long curling hair was growing. "I *live* for you. Okay? If you and your sisters are happy, I'm happy. End of story."

"Stop," said Andi. "There's no point in creating more hostilities."

"I want to know if he *tried* to get kicked out."

"You think if I was trying to get kicked out of that school, it would have taken me till second semester, eighth grade?"

Eric walked out, and like a train behind the engine we followed him back to Renata's room. The room is purple, green, orange, red, and yellow, with many pillows and framed photographs of us.

"Type in your password, please?" Eric asked Renata.

We all made a half-circle around Renata's computer. To the left of her desk, Renata has a tremendous aquarium. She takes great care of it with no help from anyone. I buy her the fish and the supplies from a company she found on the Internet. They pack everything up, then send it by overnight mail from California. Does that girl love getting fish in the mail! From there, it's all her. Feeds, cleans, replaces. Big fish, little fish, striped fish, whiskered fish. She practices viola in front of the long, bubbling tank. Says the fish can tell when she hits a bad note.

Eric sat at Renata's computer and opened an e-mail account that he said was his.

"*Don't* ask who *any* of these are from," he said to me.

"Who are they from?" I couldn't resist asking.

He mumbled at me under his breath, a code of abbreviations.

The screen was topped with ads for dating and travel. Eric brought up an e-mail message. Mina drew close to him, pronounced the line of words:

We miss you Eric! Come back soon! School isnt the same without you!

She didn't laugh. The fish swam slowly as if along a track.

"Well, that's a nice message," I said, gripping the chair behind Eric's shoulders. "When did you get that? Has he shown you this message before, Scout? Andi?"

He hadn't shown anyone.

The climate in the room was a comfortable 70 degrees, and there was a clean scent of freshly folded cotton.

"What's your point?" I said.

Eric clicked, clicked, clicked and brought up another e-mail.

"The last one was from Tuesday, March 7," he said. "Here's the date," he pointed.

This next e-mail, also from March 7, said:

We love you Eric. Straight from the heart.

"Well, that's nice, too," I said.

He brought up another, from March 8:

Somebody wants you. Somebody REALLY wants you.

Then, from March 9:

I REALLY REALLY REALLY want Eric Langer. Bad.

Then another from March 9:

Eric Langer you rock star! You make me go deep like a woman. Can you feel me?

Then yet another from March 9:

Eric boy, Eliezer, Eliezer ben Kalman, are you thinking of me?
I know your thinking of me. Let me teach you everything you want to know about the ways of heaven...

Eric clicked off the e-mail account with a frozen face, and brought back Renata's original screen, which was a photograph of her fish tank.

"Are you happy?" he said. "Because I'm happy if you're happy."

Andi's face had become outraged. Outraged and almost sickened. Sickened and dark. The markings under her eyes were like dark green leaves.

"Do you think kids at school were sending you messages on the computer while you were suspended?" she asked.

"Do I *think*?"

"Who was it?" I demanded.

"Who wasn't it?"

"Speak in answers, Eric," Renata said. "You can."

"What they do is not hard. They set up free outside accounts using the school computers, so you can't trace the e-mails to a single person. Not that it matters. Everyone at that school is the same person anyway."

"Please don't say that," Andi said. "We don't need to group individuals that way, even when we're upset. I can see that your feelings are hurt."

"My feelings are NOT HURT!" Eric blasted, at a volume and preciseness of articulation that were unusual for him. "These people deserve whatever happens to them. If you can't see that, it's not my problem."

"*Who* deserves?" I demanded again. "Were girls messing with you? T.B.S.? Or was it that Westenthal from Jacksonville? Do you think he did this with girls looking on, giggling? Or are there other boys? Don't tell me Dickie or Lowell did this."

I saw Eric's stern mouth and his periwinkle shirt and his single-striped cap and the five-colored decor of Renata's room and the fish tank.

"This is the last thing I'm ever saying about this and then none of you will ever see any e-mail I get ever again, including other ones I have," Eric said. He was looking at the photograph of the fish tank on Renata's screen. "At the end of Megilat Esther," he said, quite seriously, "after Mordecai and Esther are the big heroes and Haman goes down, what do the Jews do?"

"Celebrate," Renata said.

"Wrong," Eric answered. "First they go and kill 75,000 people who were plotting against them. Then they celebrate. Why? Because that's how it is. You plot against me, I kill you."

"Yeah," Mina agreed.

My son lowered his new striped cap across his forehead.

"Eric, Haman and many of the people in that land were plotting our extermination," Andi said. "They wanted to eliminate every trace of us from the earth. Do you remember that part of the story?"

"Yes," he said.

"Then what are you telling us?"

She reminded him of the story's larger messages of redemption, courage, cross-cultural unity, and freedom.

"Was somebody at school plotting your extermination, Eric?" Renata asked.

"They don't need to," he said. "I'm dead."

Eric walked out of the house. I hurried and put on shoes and went after him. I was sure he had gone up to the woods, maybe into the woods, and I searched up there under the poplars, calling and whistling, but I couldn't find him. I took out the car and drove up the lane. I combed the development community, court after circle after court after lane. I again whistled for him, a whistle he would recognize. Finally, I drove out of the development community and over along the river of white-blooming trees. Even the branches of the willows had caught fire. The river was quiet. I caught up to him in the car. I had his swim trunks on the seat.

Pulling over along the riverside, I called out the window, "Come on, boy. Let's go somewhere. You're not dead." He was walking slowly against the direction of the current. I stopped the car, reached over and opened the door for him. There was a clump of witch hazel behind him on the bank. He looked at me from the corner of one eye, and I didn't lose his gaze. "You're the farthest thing from dead," I said. "You're a beautiful creature of God." He stood there like a bird whose heart you can see beating in his cheek. I waited for him. I waited for him to make a move.

Jonathan Blum grew up in Miami and
graduated from UCLA and the Iowa Writers'
Workshop. His short stories have appeared
in *Green Mountains Review*, *Gulf Coast*,
Northwest Review, *Other Voices*, *Playboy*, and
elsewhere. He has taught fiction writing
at the University of Iowa and at Drew
University, and is the recipient of a Michener-
Copernicus Society of America Award and a
grant from the Helene Wurlitzer Foundation.
He lives in Los Angeles.

**RESCUE
+PRESS**